THE
HEARTBREAKER
PRINCE

THE HEARTBREAKER PRINCE

BY

KIM LAWRENCE

MILLS
BOON

First published in Great Britain 2014
by Mills & Boon, an imprint of Harlequin (UK) Limited,
Large Print edition 2014
Eton House, 18-24 Paradise Road,
Richmond, Surrey, TW9 1SR

© 2014 Kim Lawrence

ISBN: 978-0-263-24105-1

Harlequin (UK) Limited's policy is to use papers that are natural, renewable and recyclable products and made from wood grown in sustainable forests. The logging and manufacturing processes conform to the legal environmental regulations of the country of origin.

Printed and bound in Great Britain
by CPI Antony Rowe, Chippenham, Wiltshire

For Barbara, thanks for all your support.

CHAPTER ONE

HANNAH WAS NOT sleeping when the key turned in the lock. Apart from a few snatched moments she had not slept for forty-eight hours straight but she was lying down, her eyes closed against the fluorescent light above her head, when the sound made her sit bolt upright and swing her legs over the side of the narrow metal bed.

She made a few frantic attempts to smooth her tousled hair back from her face and clasped her shaking hands on her lap. She was able to mould her expression into a mask of composure, but recognised that it was no longer a matter of *whether* she lost it and cracked wide open, but *when*. For now at least she cared about maintaining an illusion of dignity.

She blinked against the threat of tears that stung like hot gravel pricking the backs of her eyes. Gouging her teeth into her plump lower lip, she found the pain helped her focus as she lifted her chin and pulled her shoulders back, drawing her narrow back ramrod straight. For the moment at least she was determined she wouldn't give the bastards the satisfaction of seeing her cry.

This was what happened when you tried to prove...*prove*...what? And to whom? The tabloids? Your father? Yourself...?

She took a deep breath. Focus on the facts, Hannah. The fact is you messed up big time! You should have accepted what everyone else thinks: you are not meant for serious thoughts or fieldwork. Stick to your safe desk job, and your perfect nails... She curled her fingers to reveal a row of nails bitten below the quick and swallowed a bubble of hysteria.

'Stiff upper lip, Hannah.'

She had always thought that was an absurd phrase.

About as absurd as thinking working a desk job for a charity qualified you for working in the field in any capacity!

'I won't let you down.'

Only she had.

She lowered her eyelids like a shield and tensed in every nerve fibre of her body just before the door swung in. Focusing on the wall, she uttered the words that had become almost a mantra.

'I'm not hungry, but I require a toothbrush and toothpaste. When can I see the British consul?'

She wasn't expecting a straight answer. She hadn't had one to this, or any of the other questions she had asked, since she had been arrested on the wrong side of the border. Geography never had been her strong point. No answers, but there had been questions, many questions, the same questions over and over again. Questions and unbelieving silences.

Humanitarian aid did not translate into Quagani military speak. She told them she was not a spy and she had never belonged to a political party, and when they tried to refute her claim with a picture of her waving a banner at a protest to stop the closure of a local village infant school, she laughed—perhaps ill-advisedly.

When they weren't calling her a spy they were accusing her of being a drug runner. The evidence they used to illustrate this was boxes of precious vaccines that were now useless because they had clearly not been kept refrigerated.

For the first day she had clung to her belief that she had nothing to worry about if she told the truth. But now she couldn't believe she had ever been so naïve.

Thirty-six hours had passed, the news hadn't even made the headlines, and the diplomatic cogs had not even thought about turning when the King of Surana picked up his phone and dialled his counterpart in a neighbouring country, Sheikh Malek Sa'idi.

Two very different men stood awaiting the outcome of that conversation, and both had a vested interest.

The older was in his early sixties, of moderate height with a straggly beard and shaggy salt-and-pepper hair that curled on his collar and stuck up in tufts around his face. With his tweed jacket and comically mismatched socks, he had the look of a distracted professor.

But his horn-rimmed glasses hid eyes that

were sharp and hard, and his unkempt hair covered a brain that, combined with risk-taking inclinations and a liberal measure of ruthlessness, had enabled him to make and lose two fortunes by the time he was fifty.

Right now he stood once more on the brink of either major success or financial ruin, but his mind was not focused on his financial situation. There was one thing in the world that meant more to Charles Latimer and that was his only child. In this room, behind closed doors, his poker face had gone, leaving only a pale and terrified parent.

The other man wore his raven-black hair close cropped, and his olive-toned skin looked gold in the light that flooded the room through massive windows that looked out over a courtyard. He was several inches over six feet tall, with long legs and broad shoulders that had made him a natural for the rowing teams at school and university. Rowing was not a career in his uncle's eyes, so his first Olympics had been his last. He had gold to show for it, even if the medal lay forgotten in a drawer somewhere. He liked to push himself, he liked winning, but he did not value prizes.

Charles Latimer's restless, hand-wringing pacing contrasted with this younger man's immobility—although he was motionless apart from the spasmodic clenching of a muscle in the hollow of one lean cheek, there was an edgy, explosive quality about him.

This man was of a different generation from the anguished parent—it was actually his thirtieth birthday that day. This was not the way he had planned to celebrate, though nothing in his manner hinted at this frustration. He accepted that his feelings were secondary to duty, and duty was bred into his every bone and sinew.

He got up suddenly, his actions betraying a tension that his expression concealed. Tall and innately elegant, he walked to the full-length window, his feet silent on the centuries-old intricate ceramic tiles. Fighting a feeling of claustrophobia, he flung open the window, allowing the sound of the falling water in the courtyard below to muffle his uncle's voice. The air was humid, heavy with the scent of jasmine, but there was no sign of the dust storm that had blown up after he had landed.

It was a good twenty degrees hotter than it would have been in Antibes. Through half-closed eyes he saw Charlotte Denning, her lithe, tanned body arranged on a sun lounger by the infinity pool, a bottle of champagne on ice, ready to fulfil her promise of a special birthday treat.

Recently divorced and enjoying her freedom, she was making up for a year spent married to a man who did not share her sexual appetites.

In short she was pretty much his ideal woman.

She would be angry at his no-show and later, when she found out the reason, she would be even angrier—not that marriage would put him out of bounds. Knowing Charlotte, he thought it might even add an extra illicit thrill.

There would be no thrills for him. Marriage would put the Charlottes of this world off-limits. He had his memories to keep him warm. The ironic curve of his lips that accompanied the thought flattened into a hard line of resolve. He would marry because it was his duty. For a lucky few duty and desire were one and the same… Once he had considered himself one of the lucky ones.

He took a deep breath of fragrant air, and closed the window, refusing to allow the insidious tendrils of resentment and self-pity to take hold. If he ever thought he'd got a bad deal he simply reminded himself that he was alive. Unlike his little niece, Leila, the baby who might have become his, had things been different. She died when the plane that was carrying her and her parents crashed into the side of a mountain, killing all on board, starting an avalanche of speculation and changing his future for ever.

He *had* a future, one he had inherited from Leila's father. Since becoming the heir and not the spare he had not thought about marriage except as something that would happen and sooner rather than later. With limited time he had set about enjoying what there was of it and in his determined pursuit of this ambition he had gained a reputation. At some point someone had called him the Heartbreaker Prince, and the title had stuck.

And now a freak set of circumstances had conspired to provide him with a ready-made bride who had a reputation to match his own. There would be no twelve-month marriage for him; it was a life sentence to Heartless Hannah. Those tabloids did so love their alliteration.

'It is done.'

Kamel turned back and nodded calmly. 'I'll set things in motion.'

As the King put the phone back down on its cradle Charles Latimer shocked himself and the others present by bursting into tears.

It took Kamel slightly less than an hour to put arrangements in place and then he returned to give the two older men a run-through of the way he saw it happening. As a courtesy he got the plan signed off by his uncle, who nodded and turned to his old college friend and business partner.

'So we should have her with you by tonight, Charlie.'

Kamel could have pointed out that more factually she would be with *him*, but he refrained.

It was all about priorities: get the girl out, then deal with the consequences.

Kamel felt obliged to point out the possibility he had not been able to factor in. Not that this was a deal-breaker—in life sometimes you just had to wing it and he was confident of his ability to do so in most situations. 'Of course, if she's hysterical or—'

'Don't worry, Hannah is tough and smart. She catches on quick. She'll walk out of there under her own steam.'

And now he was within moments of discovering if the parental confidence had been justified.

He doubted it.

Kamel thought it much more likely the man had not allowed himself to believe anything else. Clearly he had indulged the girl all her life. The chances of a spoilt English society brat lasting half a day in a prison cell before she fell apart were slender at best.

So having been fully prepared for the worst, he should have been relieved to find the object of his rescue mission wasn't the anticipated hysterical wreck. For some reason the sight of this slim, stunningly beautiful woman—sitting there on the narrow iron cot with its bare mattress, hands folded in her lap, head tilted at a confident angle, wearing a creased, shapeless prison gown with the confidence and poise of someone wearing a designer outfit—did not fill him with relief, and definitely not admiration, but a blast of anger.

Unbelievable! On her behalf people were moving heaven and earth and she was sitting there acting as though the bloody butler had entered the room! A butler she hadn't even deigned to notice. Was she simply too stupid to understand the danger of her position or was she so used to Daddy rescuing her from unpleasant situations that she thought she was invulnerable?

Then she turned her head, the dark lashes lifting from the curve of her smooth cheek, and Kamel realised that under the cool blonde Hitchcock heroine attitude she was scared witless. He took a step closer and could almost smell the tension that was visible in the taut muscles around her delicate jaw, and the fine mist of sweat on her pale skin.

He frowned. He'd save his sympathy for those who deserved it. Scared or not, Hannah Latimer did not come into that category. This was a mess of her own making.

It was easy to see how men went after her, though, despite the fact she was obviously poison. He even experienced a slug of attraction himself—but then luckily she opened her mouth. Her voice was as cut glass as her profile, her attitude a mixture of disdain and superiority, which could not have won her any friends around here.

'I must demand to see the—' She stopped, her violet-blue eyes flying wide as she released an involuntary gasp. The man standing there was not holding a tray with a plate of inedible slop on it.

There had been several interrogators but always the same two guards, neither of whom spoke. One was short and squat, and the other was tall and had a problem with body odour—after he had gone the room was filled with a sour smell for ages.

This man was tall too, very tall. She found herself tilting her head to frame all of him; be-

yond height there was no similarity whatsoever
to her round-shouldered, sour-smelling jailors.
He wasn't wearing the drab utilitarian khaki of
the guards or the showy uniform with gold ep-
aulettes of the man who sat in on all the inter-
rogations.

This man was clean-shaven and he was wearing snowy white ceremonial desert robes. The
fabric carried a scent of fresh air and clean male
into the enclosed space. Rather bizarrely he carried a swathe of blue silk over one arm. Her
round-eyed, fearful stare shifted from the in-
congruous item to his face.

If it hadn't been for the slight scar that stood
out white on his golden skin, and the slight off-
centre kink in his nose, he might have been
classed as pretty. Instead he was simply beautiful… She stared at his wide, sensual mouth
and looked away a moment before he said in a
voice that had no discernible accent and even
less warmth, 'I need you to put this on, Miss
Latimer.'

The soft, sinister demand made her guts clench

in fear. Before she clamped her trembling lips together a whisper slipped through. 'No!'

This man represented the nightmare she had kept at bay and up to this point her treatment had been civilised, if not gentle. She had deliberately not dwelt on her vulnerability; she hadn't seen another woman since her arrest, and she was at the mercy of men who sometimes looked at her... The close-set eyes of the man who sat in on the interviews flashed into her head and a quiver of disgust slid through her body.

People in her situation simply vanished.

Staring at the blue fabric and the hand that held it as if it were a striking snake, she surged to her feet—too fast. The room began to swirl as she struggled to focus on the silk square, bright against the clinical white of the walls and tiled floor...blue, white, blue, white...

'Breathe.' Her legs folded as he pressed her down onto the bed and pushed her head towards her knees.

The habit of a lifetime kicked in and she took refuge behind an air of cool disdain.

'I don't need a change of clothing. I'm fine

with this.' She clutched the fabric of the baggy shift that reached mid-calf with both hands and aimed her gaze at the middle of his chest.

Two large hands came to rest on her shoulders, stopping the rhythmic swaying motion she had been unaware of, but not the spasms of fear that were rippling through her body.

Kamel was controlling his anger and resentment: he didn't want to be here; he didn't want to be doing this, and he didn't want to feel any empathy for the person who was totally responsible for the situation, a spoilt English brat who had a well-documented history of bolting at the final hurdle.

Had she felt any sort of remorse for the wave of emotional destruction she'd left in her wake? Had her own emotions ever been involved? he wondered.

Still, she hadn't got off scot-free. Some enterprising journalist had linked the car smash of her first victim with the aborted wedding.

Driven over the Edge, the headline had screamed, and the media had crucified Heartless Hannah. Perhaps if she had shown even a scrap of emotion they might have softened when it turned out that the guy had been over the drink-drive limit when he drove his car off a bridge, but she had looked down her aristocratic little nose and ignored the flashing cameras.

In London at the time, he had followed the story partly because he knew her father and partly because, like the man who had written off his car, Kamel knew what it felt like to lose the love you planned to spend your life with. Not that Amira had dumped him—if he hadn't released her she would have married him rather than cause him pain. She had been everything this woman was not.

And yet it was hard not to look into that grubby flower-like face, perfect in every detail, and feel a flicker of something that came perilously close to pity. He sternly squashed it.

She deserved everything that was going to happen to her. If there was any victim in this it was him. Luckily he had no romantic illusions about marriage, or at least his. It was never going to be a love match—he'd loved and lost and disbelieved the popular idea that this was better than not to have loved at all. Still, it was a mistake he would not make in the future. Only an imbecile would want to lay himself open to that sort of pain again. A marriage of practicality suited him.

Though Kamel had imagined his bride would be someone whom he could respect.

Why couldn't the brainless little bimbo have found meaning in her life by buying some shoes? Even facing financial collapse, Kamel was sure Daddy dear would have bought her the whole shop. Instead she decided to become an angel of mercy. While he could see the selfish delusion that had led her to do this, he couldn't understand why any legitimate medical charity would have taken her on, even on a voluntary basis.

'I asked you to put this on, not take anything off.' Kamel let out a hissing sound of irritation as she sat there looking up at him like some sort of sacrificial virgin…though there was nothing even vaguely virginal about Miss Hannah Latimer, and that quality was about the only one he didn't have a problem with in his future bride!

Digging deep into reserves she didn't know she had, Hannah got to her feet.

'If you touch me I will report you and when I get out of here—' Don't you mean *if,* Hannah? '—I'm going to be sick.'

'No, you are not,' Kamel said. 'If you want to get out of here do as I say so put the damned thing on.'

Breathing hard, staring at him with wide eyes, she backed away, holding her hands out in a warning gesture. 'If you touch me in an inappropriate way...' You'll what, Hannah? Scream? And then who will come running?

'I promise you, angel, that sex is the last thing on my mind and if it was...' His heavy-lidded eyes moved in a contemptuous sweep from her feet to her face before he added, 'I'm not asking you to strip.' He enunciated each scathing word slowly, the words very clear despite the fact he had not raised his voice above a low menacing purr since he'd come in. 'I'm asking you to cover up.'

Hannah barely heard him. The nightmare images she had so far kept at bay were crowding in.

Kamel had had a varied life, but having a woman look at him as though he were all her nightmares come true was a first. Conquering a natural impulse to shake her rather than comfort her, he struggled to inject some soothing quality into his voice as he leaned in closer. 'Your father says to tell you that…' He stopped and closed his eyes. What was the name of the damned dog? His eyes opened again as it came to him. 'Olive had five puppies.'

It had been a last thought: I need a detail, something that a stranger wouldn't know. Something that will tell her I'm one of the good guys.

Hannah froze, her wild eyes returning to his face at the specific reference to the rescue dog she had adopted.

'Yes, I'm the cavalry—' he watched as she took a shuddering sigh and closed her eyes '—so just do as you're told and cover up.' His glance moved to the honey-blonde tresses that were tangled and limp. 'And be grateful you're having a bad-hair day.'

Hannah didn't register his words past cavalry; her thoughts were whirling. 'My father sent you?'

She gave a watery smile. Her father had come through! She exhaled and sent up a silent thank you to her absent parent.

She took the fabric and looked at it. What did he expect her to do with it? 'Who are you?'

Possibilities buzzed like a restless bee through her head. An actor? Some sort of mercenary ? A corrupt official? Someone willing to do anything for money or the adrenalin buzz?

'Your ticket out of here.'

Hannah tilted her head in acknowledgement. The important thing was he had successfully blagged or bribed his way in here and represented a shot at freedom.

Her jaw firmed. Suddenly she felt the optimism she had not allowed herself to feel during her incarceration. It had been an hour to hour— hard to believe there had only been forty-eight, but then, in a room illuminated twenty-four-seven by the harsh fluorescent light, it was hard to judge time.

'Is Dad…?'

He responded to the quiver of hope in her voice with a stern, 'Forget your father and focus. Do not allow yourself to become distracted.'

The tone enabled her to retain her grip on her unravelling control. He had the shoulders but he clearly had no intention of offering them up for tears, which was fine by her. If a girl didn't learn after two failed engagements that the only person she could rely on was herself, she deserved everything she got!

'Yes…of course.'

Her fingers shook as she took the shimmering blue fabric. It fell in a tangled skein on the floor, the fabric unravelling… Just like me, she thought.

She took a deep breath and released it, slowly able to lift her chin and meet his gaze with something approaching composure as she asked, 'What do you want me to do?'

Kamel felt an unwilling stab of admiration.

'I want you to keep your mouth closed, your head covered, and follow my lead.'

He bent forward and took the fold of fabric

from her fingers. The fabric billowed out of his hands and she was suddenly swathed in the stuff, covering her head and most of the ugly shift.

He stood back to see the effect, then nodded and threw the remaining fabric over her shoulder. His hand stayed there, heavy, the contact more reassuring than his stern stare.

'Can you do that?'

'Yes,' she said, hoping it was true.

'Right. You are going to leave here and you are going to do so with your head held high. Just channel all your…just be yourself.'

She blinked up into his dark eyes, noticing the little silver flecks, and struggled to swallow a giggle—she knew that once she gave in to hysteria that was it.

'And they are just going to let us out?' His confidence bordered the insane but maybe that was a good thing for someone in charge of a jail break.

'Yes.'

'I don't know why they let you just walk in here but—'

'They let me just walk in here because to refuse me access would have caused offence and they have a lot of ground to make up.' They could arrest, interrogate and imprison a foreign national on charges that carried the death penalty, but not the bride-to-be of the heir to the Suranian throne.

Maybe if she had chosen another moment to stray across the border his uncle's influence alone would have been enough to gain her freedom, but with impeccable timing Hannah Latimer had wandered into an armed border patrol at a time when the ruling family of Quagani was politically vulnerable. Accused by rival factions of being unable to protect the country's interests against foreign exploitation, the royals had responded by instigating a draconian zero-tolerance policy: no second chances, no leniency, no special cases...*almost*.

His uncle had not ordered, he had not played the duty card—instead he had spoken of a debt he owed Charles Latimer and asked with uncharacteristic humility if Kamel would be willing to marry Hannah Latimer.

'She is not ideal,' the King admitted, 'and not the person I would have wanted for you, but I'm sure with guidance… She was a lovely child, as I recall. Very like her mother, poor Emily.' He sighed.

'She grew up.'

'It is your decision, Kamel.'

This was the first thing ever asked of him by his uncle—who was not just his King but also the man who had stepped in after his father's death and treated him as his own son. Kamel's response had never been in doubt.

Hannah heard the irony in her rescuer's voice but didn't have a clue what it meant. 'I don't understand a word you're saying.' Though he said it in a voice that had a tactile shiver-down-your-spine quality.

'You will.' Despite the smile that went with the words, she sensed an underlying threat that was echoed in the bleakness of his stare.

'Look, no one is about to ask you anything, but

if they do, don't say anything. Burst into tears or something.'

That would not require much effort. The walking might, though—her knees felt like cotton wool.

'Just pretend you're running away from some sucker at the altar.'

Her shocked violet eyes widened to their fullest extent. The reputation she pretended not to care about had followed her to a jail halfway around the world. Ironically she had come here in the hope of rebuilding her reputation, or at least escaping the cameras.

'I believe you've had some practice,' he murmured before seamlessly raising his voice from the soft, for-her-ears-only undertone, to an authoritative command to the prison guards.

The words were unintelligible to her but the effect was magic. The guards she recognised stood either side of the open door, their heads bowed. Along the corridor there were uniformed figures standing to attention.

The man beside her spoke and the guards bowed lower. Hannah stared, astonished—it wasn't just their reaction; it was the man himself. He seemed to have assumed a totally new persona, and it fitted him as well as the flowing robes. He was clearly immersing himself in his role; even his body language had changed. The arrogance was still there but it was combined with an air of haughty authority as he strode along, shortening his step so that she could keep pace.

What the hell was happening?

She had expected to be smuggled out of some back entrance, not to receive the red-carpet treatment.

Like a sleepwalker, Hannah allowed her tall escort to guide her down the corridor. Nobody looked directly at her or her companion as they walked past. The silence was so intense she could feel it.

Outside, the heat hit her—it was like walking into a shimmering wall, but the sun was infinitely preferable to the ten-foot-square, white-walled cell. It was the thought of being discovered and ending up back there and not the temperature that brought Hannah out in a cold sweat.

A leashed guard dog began to bark, straining at the lead as they walked on. Could dogs really smell fear? As his handler fought to control the animal the man beside her turned, clicked his fingers and looked at the dog, who immediately dropped down on his belly and whimpered.

Neat trick, Hannah thought, momentarily losing her balance as a jet flew low overhead. She had heard the sound before many times over the last days but it was a lot quieter in her cell.

'I'm fine,' she mumbled as the hand on her elbow slid to her waist. In that moment of contact she registered the fact that his body had no give—it was all hard muscle. For a moment she enjoyed an illusion of safety before she was released.

Hannah, who had been totally disorientated when she had arrived in darkness, realised for the first time that she had been incarcerated on a military base.

Almost as if some of his strength had seeped into her, she felt more confident, enabling her to adopt a fatalistic attitude when they were approached by a mean-looking man with shoulders the size of a hangar, dressed similarly to the man she struggled to keep pace with.

Hannah wanted to run, every survival instinct she had was screaming at her to do so, but the hand that reached down and took her own had other ideas. Her escort had stopped when he saw the other man and waited. Under her blue silk and grubby shift Hannah sucked in a shaky breath and began to sweat—but the hand that held her own was cool and dry.

'This is Rafiq.'

So clearly friend, not foe. She managed a shaky half-smile when the big man acknowledged her presence with a respectful tip of his covered head. He responded with calm, one-word replies to the questions her escort threw at him, even earning a tight smile that might have been approval.

Hannah, who hadn't been able to follow a word, was unable to restrain herself. 'Is everything all right?'

'You mean are you about to escape justice?'

'I'm innocent!'

Her protest drew a sardonic smile from her rescuer. She had the impression he wasn't her greatest fan, but she didn't mind so long as he got her out of here.

'We are all guilty of something, angel. As the man said, there's no such thing as a free meal, but, yes, your taxi awaits.'

Hannah spun to face the direction in which he had nodded and saw a jet with a crest on the side that seemed vaguely familiar.

CHAPTER TWO

AT THE SIGHT of the private jet Hannah felt her heart race. Her anticipation of imminent escape and the possibility that her father was inside waiting were mingled with the equally powerful conviction that any minute someone would catch on. To be caught when freedom was literally within sight, touch and smell would be so much harder than if she had never hoped.

'Keep it together.'

She turned her head sharply, the action causing the silk to fall away from her cheek. She could not believe he could look so relaxed. Did the man have ice in his veins? No—she remained conscious of the warmth of his guiding hand on her elbow.

Hannah twitched the silk back into place and in doing so caught sight of someone who was approaching across the tarmac. Her eyes widened to large pools of blue terror in a face that had become dramatically pale.

'Do not run.'

Fear clutched her belly. 'He...'

Kamel watched as she licked her dry lips. Her eyes were darting from side to side like a cornered animal seeking an avenue of escape, but they kept moving back to the army colonel who carried a cane and an air of self-importance as he approached them, flanked by a small armed guard.

It didn't take a second for Kamel to experience a flash of vengeful rage that reminded him strongly of a time in his youth when, after escaping the security that he hated, he had encountered three much older boys in a narrow side street. He had not known at first what was lying on the ground there, but he had seen one boy aim a kick at it, and they had all laughed. It was the laughter he had reacted to with sheer, blinding, red-mist rage.

He had arrived back at the palace later, looking worse than the poor stray dog the trio had been systematically kicking the hell out of. He had freed the dog in the end, not by physical means but by offering them the ring he wore.

His father, the antithesis of a tyrannical parent, had been more bemused than angry when he'd discovered the ring was gone.

'You gave a priceless heirloom for this flea-ridden thing?' He had then progressed to remind Kamel how important breeding was.

It was an important lesson, not in breeding but in negotiation. In a tight situation, it was often a clear head rather than physical force that turned the tide. He controlled his instinctive rage now. Summing up the man in a glance, he knew he had come across the kind before many times: a bully who took pleasure from intimidating those he controlled.

'Did he interrogate you?'

Hannah shivered, not from the ice in Kamel's voice, but the memory.

'He watched.' And tapped a cane on the floor, she thought, shivering again as she remembered the sound. The man's silence had seemed more threatening to her than the men who asked the questions. That and the look in his eyes.

Kamel's jaw was taut, and his voice flat. 'Lift your head up. He can't do a thing to you.'

'Highness, I am here to offer our sincere apologies for any misunderstanding. I hope it has not given Miss Latimer a dislike of our beautiful country.'

And now it was his turn.

His turn to smile and lie through his teeth. It was a talent that he had worked on to the point where his diplomacy looked effortless even though it frequently veiled less civilised instincts.

He uncurled his clenched fingers, unmaking the fists they had instinctively balled into, but he was spared having to produce the words that stuck in his throat by sudden activity around the waiting jet.

As something came screaming down towards them, one man raised a pistol. Kamel, who had the advantage of faster reflexes, reached casually out and chopped the man's arm, causing him to drop the gun to the ground. It went off, sending a bullet into a distant brick wall.

'Relax, it's just…'

He stopped as the hawk that had been flying above their heads dropped down, claws extended, straight onto the head of the uniformed colonel. His hat went flying and he covered his head protectively as the hooded hawk swooped again—this time escaping with what looked like a dead animal in his talons.

The colonel stood there, his hands on his bald head.

Releasing a hissing signal from between his teeth, Kamel extended his arm. The hawk responded to the sound and landed on his wrist.

'You are quite safe now, Colonel.' Kamel took the toupee from the bird and, holding it on one finger, extended it to the man who had curled into a foetal crouch, his head between his hands.

Red-faced, the older man rose to his feet, his dignity less intact than his face, which had only suffered a couple of superficial scratches, oozing blood onto the ground.

He took the hairpiece and crammed it on his head, drawing a smothered laugh from one of his escorts. When he spun around the men stared ahead stonily.

'That thing should be destroyed. It nearly blinded me.'

Kamel touched the jewel attached to that bird's hood. 'My apologies, Colonel. No matter how many jewels you put on a bird of prey, she remains at heart a creature of impulse. But then that is the attraction of wild things, don't you think?'

The other man opened his mouth and a grunt emerged through his clenched teeth as he bowed.

Kamel smiled. He handed back the pistol to the man who had tried to shoot it, having first emptied the barrel with a mild reproach of, 'Unwise.' He then turned to Rafiq and issued a soft-voiced command in French that Hannah struggled to make sense of.

The big man bowed his head, murmured, 'Highness,' and took Hannah's elbow.

Hannah, who had remained glued to the spot while the drama had played out around her, did not respond to the pressure.

Kamel, his dark eyes flashing warning, touched her cheek.

Like someone waking from a deep sleep, she started and lifted her blue eyes to his face. 'Go with Rafiq. I will be with you presently, my little dove.' Without waiting to see if she responded, he turned to the bleeding and humiliated colonel. 'Please forgive Emerald. She is very protective and responds when she senses danger. She is... unpredictable. But as you see—' he ran a finger down the bird's neck '—quite docile.'

Kamel could feel the effort it cost the man to smile. 'You have an unusual pet, Prince Kamel.'

Kamel produced a smile that was equally insincere. 'She is not a pet, Colonel.'

He could feel the man's eyes in his back as he walked away. Still, a poisonous stare was less painful than the bullet he would no doubt have preferred to deliver.

'No.' Hannah shook her head and refused to take the seat that she was guided to. 'Where is he?' she asked the monolith of a man who didn't react to her question. 'My father! Where is he?'

As the door closed behind him the hawk flew off Kamel's hand and onto her perch, the tinkle of bells making Hannah turn her head. 'Where is my father? I want my—'

He cut across her, his tone as bleak as winter, but not as cold and derisive as his eyes. 'You should know I have no taste for hysteria.'

'And you should know I don't give a damn.'

Kamel, who had anticipated her reaction to be of the standard 'poor little me' variety, was actually pleasantly surprised by her anger. If nothing else the girl was resilient. Just as well—as it was a quality she was going to need.

'I suppose it was too much to hope that you have learnt anything from your experience.' He arched a sardonic ebony brow. 'Like humility.'

Now wasn't that the ultimate in irony? She was being lectured on humility by a man who had just produced a master class in arrogance.

She hadn't expected to be told she'd done brilliantly or receive a pat on the back…but a lecture?

'You got me out of there, so thanks. But I'm damned if I'm going to be lectured by the hired help!' It came out all wrong. But what did it matter if he thought she was a snob? She needed to know what the hell was happening and he wouldn't even give her a straight answer.

At last she was now living down to his expectations. He peeled off his head gear, revealing a head of close-cropped raven-black hair. The austere style emphasised the classical strength of his strongly sculpted features. 'I suggest that we postpone this discussion until we are actually in the air.'

It wasn't a suggestion so much as an order, and his back was already to her. She had just spent two days in a cell experiencing a total lack of control—this man was going to give her answers!

'Don't walk away from me like that!'

Dragging a hand back and forth over his hair, causing it to stand up in spikes, he paused and turned his head towards her without immediately responding. Instead in a low aside he spoke to his massive stone-faced sidekick, who bowed his head respectfully before he whisked away—moving surprisingly quickly for such a large man.

His attentions switched back to Hannah. 'It's called prioritising, my little dove.'

Hannah felt her stomach muscles tighten at the reminder that the last hurdle was still to be negotiated. At least most of the quivering was associated with fear. Some of it…well, it wasn't as if she were struck dumb with lust, but a little dry-mouthed maybe? Previously her fear levels had given her some protection from the aura of raw sexuality this man exuded, but she felt it even more strongly when he hooked a finger under her chin and looked down into her face for a moment before letting his hand drop away.

The contact and the deep dark stare had been uncomfortable, but now it was gone she wasn't sure what she felt. She gave her head a tiny shake to clear the low-level buzz—or was that the jet engines? She was clearly suffering the effects of an adrenalin dip; the chemical circulating in her blood had got her this far, but now she was shaking.

'Sit down, belt up and switch off your phone,'

he drawled, wondering if he hadn't been a bit too tough on her. But she acted tough, and looked... His eyes slid over the soft contours of her fine-boned face. She was possibly one of the few women on the planet who could look beautiful after two days in a ten-foot-square prison cell.

She sat down with a bump because it was preferable to falling. Had she thanked him yet?

'Thank you.' Hannah had been brought up to be polite, after all, and he had just rescued her.

She closed her eyes and missed the look of shock on his face. As the jet took off she released a long, slow sigh and didn't open her eyes again, even when she felt the light brush of hands on her shoulder and midriff as a belt was snapped shut.

Was it possible that she had jumped from the proverbial frying pan straight into...what? And with whom? It was only the knowledge that he carried the personal message from her father that had stopped her tipping over into panic as her imagination threatened to go wild on her.

'If you would like anything, just ask Rafiq. I have some work to do.'

She opened her eyes in time to see her rescuer shrug off his imposing desert robes to reveal a pale coffee-coloured tee shirt and black jeans. The resulting relaxed image should have been less imposing, but actually wasn't—even though he appeared to have shrugged off the icy-eyed hauteur that had reduced the aggressive colonel to red-faced docility.

He might be dressed casually, his attitude might be relaxed when he glanced her way, but this didn't change the fact that he exuded a level of sexuality that was unlike anything she had ever encountered.

He took a couple of steps, then turned back, his dark, dispassionate stare moving across her face. So many questions—Hannah asked the one that she felt took priority. 'Who are you?'

His mouth lifted at one corner but the dark silver-flecked eyes stayed coolly dispassionate as he responded, 'Your future husband.'

Then he was gone.

CHAPTER THREE

'IS THERE ANYTHING I can get for you?'

The words roused Hannah from her semi catatonic state. She surged to her feet and flung the man mountain before her a look of profound scorn before pushing past him into the adjoining cabin, which contained a seating area and a bed on which her tall, rude rescuer was stretched out, one booted foot crossed over the other, his forearm pressed across his eyes.

'I thought you were working.'

'This is a power nap. I want to look good in the wedding photos.'

Breathing hard, she stood there, hands on her hips, glaring at his concealed face—noticing as she did the small bloody indentations on the sides of his wrist, presumably from where the hawk had landed on his bare skin.

'Can you be serious for one moment, please?'

He lifted a dark brow and with a long-suffering sigh dropped his arm. Then, in one sinuous motion, he pulled himself up into a sitting position and lowered his feet to the ground.

He planted his hands on his thighs and leaned forward. 'I'm all yours. Shoot.'

Hannah heard *shoot* and shuddered, recalling the scene on the tarmac where but for his lightning reflexes there might have been more than one bullet discharged—a disaster narrowly averted.

'You should put some antiseptic on those.'

His dark brows twitched into a puzzled line.

She pointed to his arm. 'The bird.' She angled a wary glance at the big bird. 'You're bleeding.'

He turned his wrist and shrugged in an irritatingly tough fashion. 'I'll live.'

'I, on the other hand, am feeling a little insecure about being on a plane with a total stranger going...' she gave an expressive shrug '...God knows where. So do you mind filling in a few blanks?'

He nodded. She didn't sound insecure. She sounded and looked confident and sexy and in control. What would it take to make her lose it? It could be he was about to find out.

'My father sent you?'

He tipped his head in acknowledgement and she gave a gusty sigh of relief. 'He sends his love.'

'I'm sure Dad appreciates your sense of humour, but I'm a bit…'

'Uptight? Humourless?'

Her blue eyes narrowed to slits. She had very little energy left, and being angry with him was using it all up. She took a deep breath and thought, Rise above it, Hannah. People had said a lot worse about her and she'd maintained her dignity.

It was a power thing. If *they* saw it got to her *they* had the power and she lost it. It didn't matter who *they* were—school bullies, journalists—the same rule applied. If you showed weakness they reacted like pack animals scenting blood.

'I'd prefer to know what's happening, so if you could just fill me in…? Tell me where the plane is headed and then I'll let you sleep in peace.'

'Surana.'

The mention of the oil-rich desert state fired a memory. That was where she'd seen the crest on the plane before, and it fitted: her father had called in some favours. She knew he counted the King of Surana as a personal friend; the two men had met forty years earlier at the public school they had attended as boys. The friendship had survived the years—apparently the King had once dandled her on his knee but Hannah had no recollection of the event.

'So Dad will be there to meet us?'

'No, he'll be waiting at the chapel.'

Hannah fought for composure. Was this man on something? 'Hilarious.' She tried to laugh but laughing in the face of the ruthless resolve stamped on his hard-boned face was difficult. She hefted a weary sigh and reminded herself she was free. It was all up from here, once she got a straight answer from this man. 'This is not a joke that has the legs to run and run.'

His broad shoulders lifted in a shrug that suggested he didn't care. 'Look, I wish it were a joke. I have no more wish to marry you than you have me, but before you start bleating for Daddy ask yourself what you would have preferred if I'd offered you the option back there: marrying me, or spending twenty years in a boiling-hot jail where luxury is considered a tap shared by several hundred. Or even worse—'

'How does it get worse?'

'How about the death penalty?'

'That was never a possibility.' Her scorn faltered and her stomach clenched with terror. Had she really been that close? 'Was it?'

He arched a sardonic brow.

'So if I'd signed the confession…?' Her voice trailed away as she spoke until 'confession' emerged from her white lips as a husky whisper.

'You didn't.' Kamel fought the irrational feeling of guilt. He was only spelling out the ugly facts; he was not responsible. Still, it gave him no pleasure to see the shadow of terror in her wide eyes. 'So don't think about it.'

The advice brought her chin up with a snap. 'I wouldn't be thinking about it at all if you hadn't told me.'

'Maybe it's about time you faced unpleasant

facts and accepted that there are some things we cannot run away from.'

Not several thousand feet off the ground, but once they landed Hannah intended to run very fast indeed from this man. 'I'm grateful to be free, obviously, but I didn't do anything wrong.'

'You entered a sovereign state illegally, carrying drugs.'

Hannah's clenched teeth ached. His righteous attitude was really getting under her skin.

'I got lost and I was carrying medicine. Vaccines and antibiotics.'

'Morphine?'

Feeling defensive, Hannah rubbed her damp palms against her thighs. With his steely eyes and relentless delivery he was a much more effective interrogator than her captors had been. 'Yes.'

'And a camera.'

'No!'

'Isn't there a camera on your phone?'

He would have thought better of her if she had the guts to hold up her hands and take responsibility for her own actions, but that obviously wasn't her style.

'Weren't you told to stay with the vehicle if it broke down?'

How did he know? 'It was an emergency.' And that was the only reason she had been entrusted the responsibility. There simply had been no one else available.

'And you were the one on the ground and you made a tough call...fine. But now you have to take the consequences for that decision.'

Struggling to keep pace with the relentless pace of his reasoning, she shook her head. 'So I have to marry you because you rescued me? Sure, *obvious*. I should have realised.'

The bored façade and the last shades of cynical amusement in his manner fell away as he vaulted to his feet.

He towered over her, eyes blazing with contempt. She could feel the anger spilling out of him and presumably so could the bird sitting on its perch—it began to squawk and Hannah lifted her hands to her head to protect herself.

The act of soothing the spooked creature

seemed to help Kamel regain some semblance of control. 'She won't hurt you.'

Hannah dropped her hands, cast a quick sideways glance at the fascinating wild creature, and then returned her attention to the man. 'I wasn't worried about the *bird*.'

His jaw tightened in response to the pointed comment, and he stared at the mouth that delivered it…her wide, full, sexy lower lip. Hers was a mouth actually made for kissing.

'I wouldn't marry you even if you *were* sane!'

She might have a point. Wasn't it insane to be checking out her impossibly long legs? Wasn't it even more insane to actually like the fact she didn't back away from him, that her pride made her give as good as she got?

'And came gift-wrapped!' Hannah caught herself wondering how many women would have liked to unwrap him, and felt a lick of fear before she told herself that she was not one of them.

'You want facts? Fine. When we land in Surana in—' He turned his wrist and glanced at the watch that glinted against his dark skin.

'Thirty minutes. There will be a red carpet

and reception committee for Your Royal Highness,' she finished his sentence for him, and, keeping her eyes on his face, she performed a graceful bow.

He took her sarcasm at face value.

'There will be no official reception under the circumstances. Things will be low-key. We will go straight to the palace where my uncle, the King—'

Her eyes flew wide. '*King?* You're asking me to believe you're really a prince?'

He stared at her hard. 'Who did you think I was?'

'Someone my father paid to get me out of jail. I thought you were pretending to—'

'I can't decide if you're just plain stupid or incredibly naïve.' He shook his head from side to side in an attitude of weary incredulity. 'You thought all I had to do was walk in, claim to be of royal blood and all the doors would open to release you?' What alternative universe did this woman live in?

Her eyes narrowed with dislike as he threw back his head and laughed.

'What was I meant to think?'

'That you were extremely lucky you have a father who cares so much about you, a father who is waiting with my uncle and Sheikh Sa'idi of Quagani. The only reason you are not now facing the consequences of your actions is because the Sheikh has been told that you are my fiancée.'

'And he believed that?'

'I think the wedding invite swung it.'

'Well, I'm out, so job done. You can tell him the wedding's off.'

'I can see that that is the way things work in your world.' A world with no honour.

'What is that meant to mean?'

The plane hit a pocket and he braced himself as it sank and rose while she staggered and grabbed the back of a chair. 'That you step away from commitment when it suits you.'

Hannah was waiting for her stomach to find its level but this not so veiled reference to her engagements brought an angry flush to her cheeks. 'I'm fine, thanks for asking,' she murmured, rubbing the area where her wrist had banged against the chair.

He continued as though she had not spoken. 'But that is not the way it works here. My uncle feels indebted to your father and he has given his word.'

'I didn't give my word.'

'*Your word!*' he echoed with acid scorn.

She felt the burn of tears in her eyes and furiously blinked to clear them. 'I won't be lectured by you!'

'Your word means...' he clicked his fingers '...nothing. It is otherwise with my uncle. He is a man of integrity, honour. I suppose I'm speaking a foreign language to you?'

'So your uncle would be embarrassed. I'm sorry about that—'

'But not sorry enough to accept the consequences of your actions?'

Consequences...consequences... Hannah fought the urge to cover her ears. 'This is stupid. What terrible thing is going to happen if we don't get married?' Hannah hoped the question didn't give him the false impression that she would even consider this.

'I'm glad you asked that.'

He opened the laptop that lay on a table and spun it around, stabbing it with his finger. 'We are a small country but oil rich, and we have enjoyed relative political stability. Since the discovery last year of these new reserves, we are set to be even more rich.'

She pursed her lips at his lecturing tone and stuck out her chin. 'I do read an occasional newspaper.'

'Don't boast about your IQ, angel, because,' he drawled, 'stupidity is the only possible excuse for your little escapade.'

An angry hissing sound escaped her clenched teeth. 'I know the country is a shining light of political stability and religious tolerance. What I didn't know was that the ruling family had a history of insanity—but that's what happens when you marry cousins.'

'Well, you will be a new injection of blood, won't you, angel? This will happen, you know. The sooner you accept it, the easier it will be.'

Hannah bit her lip. Even her interrogators had never looked at her with such open contempt and, though she refused to admit it even to herself, it hurt. As had the headlines and the inches of gossip all vilifying her.

'Shall I tell you why?'

He waited a moment, then tipped his head, acknowledging her silence.

'We have a problem. We are landlocked and the oil needs to get to the sea.' He flicked his finger across the screen and traced a line. 'Which means we rely on the cooperation of others. The new pipeline is at present being constructed in Quagani, and it crosses three separate countries. Did you know your father is building the pipeline?'

Hannah didn't but she would have died before admitting it. 'I'm surprised they haven't already married you off to some Quagani princess to seal the deal.'

'They were going to, but she met my cousin.' Kamel had fallen in love with Amira slowly. It had been a gradual process and he'd thought it had been the same for her. Had he not seen it with his own eyes, Kamel would have laughed at the idea of love at first sight. He had tried very hard not to see it. 'When she found him...preferable, her family were fine with it because he was the heir and I was, as they say, the spare.'

'Then where is the problem? If your families are linked they're not going to fall out.'

'He died...she died...their baby died.' The only thing that linked the rulers now was shared grief and a need to blame someone.

Like a sandcastle hit by a wave, Hannah's snooty attitude dissolved. Despite some throat-clearing her voice was husky as she said softly, 'I'm so sorry. But my father wouldn't force me to marry for any amount of money.'

He looked at the woman who sat there with spoilt brat written all over her pretty face.

'Has it occurred to you that your father, being human, might jump at the chance to get you off his hands? And if he did I don't think there are many who would blame him.'

'My father doesn't think of me as a piece of property.'

He might, however, think of her as a lead weight around his neck.

'Do you care for your father as much as he does you?'

'What does that mean?'

'It means if Quagani closes the new pipeline it won't just be the school programme in our country that suffers. Your father has a stake in the new refinery too.'

It was the mention of a school programme that brought a worried furrow to her brow. In her job she knew what a difference education could make. 'My father has a stake in many things.'

'My uncle let your father in on this deal as a favour. He knew of his situation.'

She tensed and then relaxed.

'What situation? Are you trying to tell me my father has lost all of his money again?'

Over the years her father's reckless, impulsive approach to business had led to dramatic fluctuations in fortune, but that was in the past. After the heart attack he had actually listened to the doctors' warnings about the danger of stress. He had *promised* her faithfully that the risky deals were a thing of the past.

'Not all of it.'

Hannah met his dark, implacable stare and felt the walls of the cabin close in. Even as she was shaking her head in denial she knew deep down that he was telling her the truth.

Kamel watched, arms folded across his chest, as the comment sank in. The prospect of being the daughter of a poor man seemed to affect her more than anything he had said so far. The idea of slumming it or being forced to make her own way in the world without the cushion of Daddy's money had driven what little colour she had out of her face.

'He has made a number of unfortunate ventures, and if the pipeline deal fails your father faces bankruptcy.'

Hannah's heart started to thud faster and her heart was healthy. *Stress*…what could be more stressful than bankruptcy? Unless it was the humiliation of telling a cathedral full of people that your daughter's wedding was off.

She had accepted her share of responsibility

for the heart attack that very few people knew about. At the time her father had sworn Hannah to secrecy, saying the markets would react badly to the news. Hannah didn't give a damn about the markets, but she cared a lot about her father. He was not as young as he liked to think. With his medical history, having to rebuild his company from scratch—what would that do to a man with a cardiac problem?

Struggling desperately to hide her concern behind a composed mask, she turned her clear, critical stare on her prospective husband and discovered as she stared at his lean, bronzed, beautiful face that she hadn't, as she had thought, relinquished all her childish romantic fantasies, even after her two engagements had ended so disastrously.

'So you have made a case for me doing this,' she admitted, trying to sound calm. 'But why *would you*? Why would you marry someone you can't stand the sight of? Are you really willing to marry a total stranger just because your uncle tells you to?'

'I could talk about duty and service,' he flung

back, 'but I would be wasting my breath. They are concepts that you have no grasp of. And my motivation is not the issue here. I had a choice and I made it. Now it is your turn.'

She sank onto a day bed, her head bent forward and her hands clenched in her lap. After a few moments she lifted her head. She'd made her decision, but she wasn't ready to admit it.

'What will happen? If we get married… after…?' She lifted a hank of heavy hair from her eyes and caught sight of her reflection in the shiny surface of a metallic lamp on the wall beside her. There had been no mirrors in her cell and her appearance had not occupied her thoughts so it took her a few seconds before she realised the wild hair attached to a haggard face was her own. With a grimace she looked away.

'You would have a title, so not only could you act like a little princess, you could actually be one, which has some limited value when it comes to getting a dinner table or theatre ticket.'

'*Princess…?*' Could this get any more surreal? The ingenuous, wide-eyed act irritated Kamel.

'Oh, don't get too excited. In our family,' he drawled, 'a title is almost obligatory. It means little.'

As his had, but all that had changed the day that his cousin's plane had gone down and he had become the Crown prince.

That was two years ago now, and there remained those conspiracy theorists who still insisted there had been a cover-up—that the royal heir and his family had been the victims of a terrorist bomb, rather than a mechanical malfunction.

There was a more sinister school of thought that had gone farther, so at a time when Kamel had been struggling with the intense grief and anger he felt for the senseless deaths—his cousin was a man he had admired and loved—Kamel had also had to deal with the fact that some believed he had orchestrated the tragedy that wiped out the heirs standing between him and the crown.

He had inherited a position he'd never wanted, and a future that, when he allowed himself to think about it, filled him with dread. He'd also inherited a reputation for bumping off anyone who got in his way.

And now he had a lovely bride—what more could a man want?

'My official residence is inside the palace. I have an apartment in Paris, and also a place outside London, and a villa in Antibes.' Would the lovely Charlotte still be there waiting? No, not likely. Charlotte was not the waiting kind. 'I imagine, should we wish it, we could go a whole year without bumping into one another.'

'So I could carry on with my life—nothing would change?'

'You like the life you have so much?'

His voice held zero inflection but she could feel his contempt. She struggled to read the expression in his eyes, but the dark silver-flecked depths were like the mirrored surface of a lake, deep and inscrutable yet strangely hypnotic.

She pushed away a mental image of sinking into a lake, feeling the cool water embrace her, close over her head. She lowered her gaze, running her tongue across her lips to moisten them.

When she lifted her head she'd fixed a cool

smile in place…though it was hard to channel cool when you knew you looked like a victim of a natural disaster. But her disaster was of her own making.

Her delicate jaw clenched at the insight that had only made her imprisonment worse. The knowledge that she was the author of her own disaster movie, that she had ignored the advice to wait until a driver was available, and then she had chosen not to stay with the vehicle as had been drilled into them.

'I like my freedom.' It had not escaped his notice that she had sidestepped his question.

'At last we have something in common.'

'So you…we…?' This was the world's craziest conversation. 'Is there any chance of a drink?' With a heavy sigh she let her head fall back, her eyes closed.

Exhausted but not relaxed, he decided. His glance moved from her lashes—fanning out across the marble-pale curve of her smooth cheeks and hiding the dark shadows beneath her eyes—to her slim, shapely hands with the bitten untidy nails. Presumably her manicure had been a victim of her incarceration.

She had some way to go before she could collapse. Would she make it? It appeared to him that she was running on a combination of adrenalin and sheer bloody-minded obstinacy. His expression clinical, he scrutinised the visible, blue-veined pulse hammering away in the hollow at the base of her throat. There was something vulnerable about it… His mouth twisted as he reminded himself that the last two dumb guys she'd left high and dry at the altar had probably thought the same thing.

'I'm not sure alcohol would be a good idea.'

Her blue eyes flew open. 'I was thinking more along the lines of tea.'

'I can do that.' He spoke to Rafiq, who had a habit of silently materialising, before turning his attention back to Hannah. 'Well, at least our marriage will put an end to your heartbreaking activities.'

'I didn't break anyone's—' She stopped, biting back the retort. She'd promised Craig—who had loved her but, it turned out, not in 'that' way—that she'd take responsibility.

'You're more like a sister to me,' Craig had told her. 'Well, actually, not like a sister because you know Sal and she's a total…no, more like a best friend.'

'Sal is my best friend,' Hannah had replied. And Sal had been, before she'd slept with treacherous Rob.

'That's why I'm asking you not to tell her I called it off. When we got engaged she got really weird, and told me she'd never ever forgive me if I hurt you. But I haven't hurt you, have I…? We were both on the rebound—me after Natalie and you after Rob.' He had patted her shoulder. 'I think you still love him.'

Somehow Hannah had loved the man who had slept his way through her friends while they were together. She had only known about Sal when she had given him back his ring after he stopped denying it.

She hated Rob now but he had taught her about trust. Mainly that it wasn't possible. Craig, who she had known all her life, was different. He was totally predictable; he would never hurt her. But she had forgotten one thing—Craig was a man.

'You know me so well, Craig.'

'So, are you all right with this?'

'I'm fine.'

'So what happens now?'

People who had never met you felt qualified to spend time and a lot of effort ripping you to shreds. 'I don't know,' she lied.

Her lips twitched as she recalled her ex-fiancé's response. Craig never had been known for his tact.

'Well, what happened last time?'

Hannah had shrugged guiltily. The last time her dad had done everything. Even though pride had stopped her revealing that her fiancé had slept with all her friends—pride and the fact that her father would have blamed himself, as Charles Latimer had introduced her to Rob and had encouraged the relationship.

The second time he'd run out of understanding. He'd been furious and dumped the whole nightmare mess in her lap. Her glance flickered

to the tall, imposing figure of her future husband and she struggled to see a way through the
nightmare he represented.

CHAPTER FOUR

THIS TIME HANNAH was aware of the man mountain before he appeared—just as they hit another
air pocket, he entered apologising for the tea he
had slopped over the tray he was carrying.

'I will get a fresh tray.'

'It'll be fine,' Kamel responded impatiently.
'We need not stand on ceremony with Miss Latimer. She is one of the family now. Considering
the nature of my trip I kept staffing down to a
minimum.' He murmured something in what she
assumed was Arabic to the other man, who left
the compartment. 'Rafiq can turn his hand to
most things but his culinary skills are limited.'
He lifted the domed lid on the plate to reveal a
pile of thickly cut sandwiches. 'I hope you like
chicken.'

'I'm not hungry,' she said dully.

'I don't recall asking you if you were hungry,

Hannah,' he returned in a bored drawl as he piled an extra sandwich onto a plate and pushed it her way.

She slung him an angry look. 'How am I meant to think about food when I'm being asked to sacrifice my freedom?' That had been her comfort after the battering her self-esteem had taken after being basically told she was not physically attractive by two men who had claimed to love her. At the very least she still had her freedom.

He smiled, with contempt glittering in his deep-set eyes.

'You will eat because you have a long day ahead of you.'

The thought of the long day ahead and what it involved drew a weak whimper from Hannah's throat. Ashamed of the weakness, she shook her head. 'This *can't* have been Dad's idea.'

She looked and sounded so distraught, so young and bewildered that Kamel struggled not to react to the wave of protective tenderness that rose up in him, defying logic and good sense.

'It was something of a committee decision and if there is an innocent victim in this it is me.'

This analysis made her jaw drop. Innocent and victim were two terms she could not imagine anyone using about this man.

'However, if I am prepared to put a brave face on it I don't see what your problem is.'

'My problem is I don't love you. I don't even know you.'

I am Kamel Al Safar, and now you have all the time in the world to get to know me.'

Her eyes narrowed. He had a smart answer for everything. 'I can hardly wait.'

'I think you're being unnecessarily dramatic. It's not as if we'd be the first two people to marry for reasons other than *love*.'

'So you're all right with someone telling you who to marry.' Sure that his ego would not be able to take such a suggestion, she was disappointed when he gave a negligent shrug.

'If I weren't, you'd still be languishing in a jail cell.'

She opened her mouth, heard the tap, tap of

the uniformed officer's stick on the floor and closed it again. 'Don't think I'm not grateful.'

He arched a brow. 'Is that so? Strange, I'm not feeling the love,' he drawled.

Her face went blank. 'There isn't any love.'

'True, but then basing a marriage on something as transitory as *love*—' again he said the word as though it left a bad taste in his mouth '—makes about as much sense as building a house on sand.'

Was this a man trying to put a positive spin on it or was he genuinely that cynical?

'Have you ever been in love?' It was a weird thing to ask a total stranger, but then this was a very weird situation.

And just as weird was the expression she glimpsed on the tall prince's face. But even as she registered the bleakness in his eyes his heavy lids half closed. When he turned to look directly at her there was only cynicism shining in the dark depths.

'I defer to you as an expert on that subject. Two engagements is impressive. Do you get engaged to every man you sleep with?'

'I'm twenty-three,' she tossed back.

He tipped his dark head. 'My apologies,' he intoned with smiling contempt. 'That was a stupid question.'

Hannah didn't give a damn if he thought she had casual sex with every man she met. What made her want to slap the look of smug superiority off his face were the double standards his attitude betrayed.

How dared a man who had probably had more notches in his bedpost than she'd had pedicures look down his nose at her?

'And this is all about money and power. You have it and you're prepared to do anything to keep it. You carry on calling it duty if it makes you feel any better about yourself, but I call it greed!'

Kamel struggled to contain the flash of rage he felt at the insult. 'Only a woman who has always had access to her rich daddy's wallet and has never had to work for anything in her life could be so scornful about money. Or maybe you're just stupid.'

Stupid! The word throbbed like an infected

wound in her brain. 'I do work.' If only to prove to all those people who called her stupid that people with dyslexia could do as well as anyone else if they had the help they needed.

'I think you might find your role is no longer available.'

'You couldn't say or think anything about me that hasn't been said,' she told him in a voice that shook with all the emotion she normally cloaked behind a cold mask. 'Thought or written. But enough about me. What's your contribution to society? I forget,' she drawled, adopting a dumb expression. 'What qualifications do you need to be a future King? Oh, that's right, an accident of birth.' She stopped and released a long fractured sigh. 'That's not what I wanted to say.'

He stared at her through narrowed eyes, resisting the possibility that a woman with feelings, that a woman who could be hurt, lurked behind the icy disdain.

'Well, what did you want to say?'

Relief rippled through her. This was not the response she had anticipated to her outburst.

'Would this marriage be a…paper one?'

'*Will*…get the tense right,' he chided. 'There will be official duties, occasions when we would be expected to be seen together.' He studied her face. 'But that isn't what you're talking about, is it?'

She gnawed on her lower lip and shook her head.

'It will be expected that we produce an heir.'

Shaken by the image that popped into her head, she looked away but not before her mind had stripped him naked. The image refused to budge, as did the uncomfortable feeling low in her belly.

'You might find it educational.'

The drawled comment made her expression freeze over; it hid her panic. 'The offer of lessons in sex is not a big selling point!' My God, he was really in for a disappointment.

His laugh cut over her words. 'I wasn't referring to your carnal education, though if you want to teach me a thing or two I have no problem.'

The riposte he had anticipated didn't come. Instead, astonishingly, she blushed. Kamel was not often disconcerted, but he was by her response.

Hannah, who had conquered many things but not her infuriating habit of blushing, hated feeling gauche and immature. From somewhere she dredged up some cool. 'So what were you referring to?'

'I'm assuming that your average lover is besotted. I'm not.'

'What, besotted or average?' Stupid question, she thought as her eyes slid down his long, lean, powerful frame—average was not a word anyone would use when referring to this man. 'I can't just jump into bed with you. I don't know you!'

'We have time.' He produced a thin-lipped smile. 'A lot of it. But relax, I don't expect our union to be consummated any time soon, if you can cope with that?'

'With what?'

'No sex.'

Her lashes came down in a concealing curtain. 'I'll manage.'

'Because your little adventures will be over. There can be no questioning the legitimacy of the heir to the throne,' he warned.

'And does the same rule apply to you?' Without waiting for him to reply she gave a snort of disgust. 'Don't answer that. But perhaps you could answer me this...'

He turned and she dropped the hand she self-consciously had extended to him. 'Do you know...' he seemed to know everything else with a few exceptions '...did they get the vaccinations to the village in time?'

The anxiety in her blue eyes was too genuine to be feigned. Perhaps the woman did have a conscience, but not one that stopped her doing exactly what she wanted, Kamel reminded himself.

'It is a pity you didn't think about the village when you decided to cross a border without papers or—'

'My Jeep broke down. I got lost.' Hating the whining note of self-justification, she bit her lip. 'Do you know? Could you find out?' The report that had reached the storage facility where she had been organising local distribution had said the infection was spreading rapidly; the death toll would be horrific if it wasn't contained.

'I have no idea.'

She watched as he moved away, not just in the physical sense to the other end of the cabin, but in every way. He tuned her out totally, appearing to be immersed in whatever was on the laptop he scrolled through.

Studying the back of his neck, she had to crane her own to see more than the top of his dark head. Hannah envied him and wished she could forget he existed. Was this a foretaste of the rest of her life? Occupying the same space when forced to, but not interacting? She had given up on romance but the thought of such a clinical union lay like an icy fist in her stomach.

He didn't even glance at her when the plane landed; he just left his seat, leaving her sitting there. It was the massive bodyguard who indicated she should follow Kamel down the aisle to the exit with one of his trademark tilts of the head.

She was between the two men as they disembarked. Hannah blinked in the bright sun—the blinds had been down in the cabin and for some reason she had expected it to be dark. She had lost all sense of time. She glanced down at her wrist and felt a pang when she remembered they had taken her watch. It was one of the few things she had that had been her mother's. When she was arrested they'd taken everything she had, including her sunglasses, and she would have given a lot for dark lenses to hide behind.

Her eyes flew wide with alarm.

'I don't have my passport!'

At the bottom of the steps he paused and looked up at her, his cold eyes moving across her face in a zero-tolerance sweep. 'You will not need your passport.'

'One of the perks of being royal?' Like the daunting armed presence and salutes, she thought, watching the suited figure who was bowing deferentially in response to what Kamel was saying.

Glad to be off his radar, she ran her tongue across her dry lips, frightened by how close to total panic she had come in that moment she'd thought that without a passport she would be denied entry. The thought of the cell she had escaped made her knees shake as she negotiated the rest of the steps and stood on terra firma.

There were three massive limos with darkened glass parked a few feet away on the concrete, waiting to whisk them away. One each? Unable to smile at her own joke in the presence of such an overt armed presence, she took a hurried step towards Kamel, who was striding across to the farthest car, only to be restrained by a heavy hand on her shoulder.

She angled a questioning look up and the massive bodyguard shook his head slowly from side to side.

She pulled herself back from another panic precipice and called after Kamel. 'You're leaving?'

She was literally sweating with her effort to project calm but she could still hear the sharp anxiety in her voice.

He turned his head and paused, his dark eyes sweeping her face. 'You'll be looked after.'

Hannah lifted her chin, ignoring the tight knot of loneliness in her chest. She hated the feeling;

she hated him. She would not cry—she would not let that damned man make her cry.

Kamel ruthlessly quashed a pang of empathy, but remained conscious of her standing there looking like some sort of sacrificial virgin as he got into the car. He resented the way her accusing blue eyes followed him, making him feel like an exploitative monster. It was illogical—he'd saved her. He hadn't expected to be hailed as a hero but he hadn't counted on becoming the villain of the piece. It was a tough situation, but life required sacrifice and compromise—a fact that she refused to recognise.

He pressed a button and the dark tinted window slid up. She could no longer see him but he could see her.

'What's happening to me?' She managed to wrench the question from her aching throat as she watched the sleek car draw away.

She had not directed the question at anyone in particular so she started when Rafiq, the man of few words, responded.

'My instructions are to take you to Dr Raini's home.'

He tipped his head in the direction of the open car door, clearly expecting her to get in. It hadn't even crossed his mind that she wouldn't.

Hannah felt a tiny bubble of rebellion. She'd had her independence taken away from her during the past few days, and she would not allow it to happen again. She would not become some decorative, docile wife producing stage-managed performances to enhance her husband's standing, only to become invisible when she was not needed.

Then show a bit of backbone, Hannah.

She lifted her chin and didn't move towards the open car door. 'I don't need a doctor.'

The big man, who looked thrown by her response, took his time before responding. 'No, you misunderstand. She is not that sort of doctor. She is a professor of philosophy at the university. She will help you dress for the ceremony, and will act as your maid of honour.'

He stood by the door but Hannah stayed where she was.

'What about my father?'

'I believe your father is to meet you at the royal chapel.'

The mention of a chapel drew her delicate brows into a bemused frown. She recalled the rest of the article in the Sunday supplement where she had garnered most of her knowledge about Surana—as well as being a peaceful melting pot of religions, the country was known for its royal family being Christian, which made them a rarity in the region.

After the car left the airport it turned onto a wide, palm-fringed boulevard where the sun glinted off the glass on the tall modern buildings that lined it. From there they entered what was clearly an older part of the city, where the roads were narrow and the design less geometric.

The screen between the front and back seat came down.

'We are nearly there, miss.'

Hannah nodded her thanks to Rafiq and realised they had entered what appeared to be a prosperous suburb. Almost immediately she had registered the air of affluence, and their car turned sharply through an open pair of high ornate gates and into a small cobbled courtyard hidden from the street by a high wall.

The driver spoke into his earpiece as the gates closed behind them and a suited figure appeared. The big bodyguard spoke to the man and then, with the manner of someone who habitually expected to find danger lurking behind every bush, he scanned the area before opening the door for her.

Hannah's feet hit the cobbles when the wide wooden door of the three-storey whitewashed house was flung open.

'Welcome. I'm Raini, Kamel's cousin.'

The professor turned out to be an attractive woman in her mid-thirties. Tall and slim, she wore her dark hair in a short twenties bob, and her smile was warm as she held out her hands to Hannah.

'I'd ask what sort of journey you had but I can see—'

The kindness and genuine warmth cut through all Hannah's defences and the tears started oozing out of her eyes. Embarrassed, she took the tissue that was pushed into her hand and blew her nose. 'I'm so sorry, I don't normally, it's just…I know I look like a nightmare.'

The woman gave her a hug and ushered her into the house, throwing a comment over her shoulder to the bodyguard as she closed the door very firmly behind them.

Hannah half expected the door to be knocked down; her respect for the woman went up when it wasn't.

'No need to apologise. If I'd been through what you have I'd be a basket case.'

'I am.' Hannah blinked. Inside the house was nothing like the exterior suggested: the décor was minimalist and the ground floor appeared to be totally open-plan.

'Of course you are.' She laid a comforting hand on Hannah's arm. 'This way,' she added, and opened a door that led into a long corridor. Several of the doors lining it were open, and it appeared to be a bedroom wing.

The older woman caught Hannah's bewildered expression. 'I know, it's bigger than it looks.' She smiled sympathetically. 'I'd love to give you the guided tour and I know you must be dead on your feet but we're on the clock, I'm afraid. Just in here.' She pushed open a door and waited for Hannah to enter ahead of her.

It was a big square room with tiled floors. One wall had French doors and another a row of fitted wardrobes. The large low platform bed was the only piece of furniture in the room.

'I know, bleak. I love clutter, not to mention a bit of glitz, but Steve is a minimalist with borderline OCD.' The thought of Steve, presumably her husband, brought a fond smile to her face.

The look reminded Hannah of what she wouldn't have, what she had refused to acknowledge she still wanted. She looked away, conscious of a pain in her chest, and sank down onto the bed. It was a long way down but she barely noticed the soft impact as she landed on the deep duvet. She lifted her hands to her face and shook her head.

'None of this should be happening.'

Watching her, the other woman gave a sympathetic grimace. 'I know this isn't how you envisioned your wedding day,' she said gently, 'but really it's not the wedding that counts. Everything that could go wrong did at mine. It's the person you're going to spend the rest of your life with that matters. How did you and Kamel meet?'

Hannah lifted her head. 'Sorry?'

The other woman misinterpreted her blank look. 'Don't worry, it's a story for another day, I'm just so glad he's found someone. All that playboy stuff, it was so *not* like him, but he isn't as bad as those awful tabloids painted him, you know.'

'I never read the tabloids,' Hannah responded honestly.

The other woman patted her hand and Hannah, who was more confused by these tantalising snippets of information than she had been before, realised two things: that his cousin thought the marriage was for real, and that she would be married to a man who, even his very fond cousin had to admit, had a horrific reputation.

'I prayed he'd recover from Amira one day, but when you lose someone that way...' She gave an expressive shrug. 'I ask myself sometimes, could I have been as noble if I knew that Steve had fallen for someone?'

For a moment a frustrated Hannah thought the flow of confidences had ended, but then Raini's voice dropped to a confidential whisper.

'Amira told me that Kamel said she'd make a beautiful queen, and that all he wanted was for her to be happy. He and Hakim were like brothers—talk about triangles.'

Hannah gave a non-committal grunt, struggling to put the people and places mentioned in context, and then she remembered what he had said: '*She found him...preferable.*' This love that Hannah was meant to be replacing was the woman who had married Kamel's cousin, only to lose her life in the plane crash that had moved Kamel up the line of succession. He had acted as though he didn't care but if his cousin had it right...? She shook her head, struggling to see the man who had showed her zero empathy caring for anyone. It was almost as strange an idea as him being rejected. Whether he wore a crown or not, Kamel was not the sort of man women ran away from.

'She would have, too.'

Hannah wrenched her wandering thoughts

back to the present and shook her head, mumbling, 'Sorry?'

'She would have made a beautiful queen. But she never got the chance…' Raini breathed a deep sigh. 'So sad.' Then, visibly pulling herself together, she produced a warm smile. 'But this is not a day for tears. *You will* make a beautiful queen, and you're marrying a man in a million.'

Hannah knew she was meant to respond. 'I would still be in the jail cell if it hadn't been for him.'

The other woman looked mistily emotional as she nodded. 'He's the man you need in an emergency. When Steve was kidnapped…' She gave her head a tiny shake and pulled open the wardrobe door. 'Like I said, Kamel is a guy in a million but patience is not one of his virtues, and my instructions are to have you on the road in thirty minutes.

'Take your pick of the dresses, Hannah.' She indicated a row of white gowns. 'They delivered a few.'

Hannah blinked at the understatement, and Raini continued to deliver the information at the same shotgun speed.

'Your father wasn't sure of your size so I got them to send them all in three sizes, but...' Her bright eyes moved in an assessing sweep up and down Hannah. 'You're an eight?'

Hannah nodded.

'Shower that way.' Her efficient mother hen nodded at a door. 'You'll find toiletries and make-up by the mirror—anything you want just yell. I'll just go and get changed into something much less comfortable.'

The shower was bliss. All the gowns were beautiful but she selected the simplest: a column with the hem and high neck heavily encrusted with beads and crystals. It fitted like a silken glove. Smooth and butter-soft, in dramatic contrast to the emotional rawness of her emotions. She took a deep breath and pulled the shattered threads of her protective composure tight about her shoulders, refusing to acknowledge the fear in her belly.

When Raini returned, looking elegant in a tailored silk trouser suit, Hannah was struggling with her hair. Freshly washed, it was evading her efforts to secure it in an elegant chignon.

'You look beautiful,' the older woman said, standing back to view her. 'I thought you might like this.'

Hannah's eyes travelled from the mist of emotional tears in the other woman's eyes to the lace veil she held out and her armour of cool detachment crumbled.

'It's beautiful,' she said, hating the fact she couldn't tell this woman who was so genuine the truth—that this marriage was all an awful sham.

'It was my grandmother's. I wore it when I was married. I thought you might like it.'

Hannah backed away, feeling even more wretched that she was playing the loving bride for this woman. 'I couldn't—it looks so delicate.'

'I insist. Besides, it will go perfectly with this.' She presented what Hannah had assumed was a clutch bag, but turned out to be a large rectangular wooden box.

'What beautiful work.' Hannah ran a finger along the intricate engraving work that covered the rosewood lid.

'Not nearly as beautiful as this.' With a magician's flourish Raini flicked the lid open. Her eyes were not on the contents, but on Hannah's face. She gave a smile as Hannah's jaw dropped.

'No, you're really kind, but I *really* couldn't wear that. It's far too precious. This is lovely,' she said, draping the lace veil over her head, 'but really, no.' She stepped back, waving her hands in a fluttering gesture of refusal.

'It's not mine...I wish.' Raini laughed, removing the tiara from its silken bed. The diamonds in the delicately wrought gold circlet glittered as she held it up. 'Kamel had it couriered over. He wants you to wear it. Let me...' Her face a mask of serious concentration, she placed the tiara carefully on top of the lace. *'Dieu,'* she breathed reverently. 'You look like something out of a book of fairy tales. You really are a princess.'

Hannah lifted her hands to remove it. 'I haven't put my hair up yet.'

'If I were you I'd leave it loose. It's very beautiful.'

Hannah shrugged. Her hairstyle was the least of her worries.

CHAPTER FIVE

HANNAH'S FIRST GLIMPSE of her future home drew a pained gasp from her lips.

'I know.' Raini was all amused sympathy. 'I'd like to tell you it's not as awe-inspiring as it looks, but actually,' she admitted, directing her critical stare at the multitude of minarets, 'it is. Even Hollywood couldn't build a set like this. The family, as you'll learn, has never been into less is more. When I lived here—'

'You lived here?' How did anyone ever relax in a setting this ostentatiously grand?

Raini gave a warm chuckle. 'Oh, my parents occupied a small attic,' she joked. 'Until Dad got posted. He's a diplomat,' she explained. 'By the time I was eighteen I'd lived in a dozen cities.' They drove under a gilded archway into a courtyard the size of a football pitch, filled with fountains. 'But nothing ever came close to this.'

Hannah believed her.

Rafiq escorted them into the building through a small antechamber that had seemed large until they stepped through the next door and entered a massive hall. The wall sconces in there were all lit, creating swirling patterns on the mosaic floor.

The awful sense of impending doom that lay like a cold stone in Hannah's chest became heavier as they followed the tall, gowned figure down a maze of marble-floored empty corridors. By the time she saw a familiar figure, she was struggling to breathe past the oppressive weight.

'Dad!'

'Hello, Hannah! You look very beautiful, child.'

Hannah struggled to hide her shock at her father's appearance. She had never seen him look so pale and haggard. Not even when he'd lain in a hospital bed attached to bleeping machines had he looked this frail. He seemed to have aged ten years since she last saw him.

Any lingering mental image of her walking into his arms and asking him to make everything right vanished as the tears began to slide down his cheeks. She had never seen her ebullient parent cry except on the anniversary of her mother's death—her birthday. On that day he always vanished to be alone with his grief, and the sight of tears now was as painful to her as a knife thrust.

Intentionally or not, it always felt as if she was the cause of his tears. If she hadn't been born the woman he loved would not have died and now this was her fault. About that much Kamel was right.

She had been doing a job that she was ill qualified to do and she'd messed up. But the consequences had not been just hers. Other people had suffered. She lifted her chin. Well, that was going to stop. She'd made the mistake and she'd take the nasty-tasting medicine, though in this instance it came in the shape of the dark and impossibly handsome and arrogant Prince of Surana.

'I thought I'd lost you,' her father cried. 'They have the death penalty in Quagani, Hannah. It was the only way we could get you out. They wanted to make an example of you, and without the King's personal intervention they would have. Kamel is a good man.'

It seemed to be a universally held opinion. Hannah didn't believe it. Nonetheless, it was clear that he had not just freed her, he had saved her life.

'I know, Dad. I'm fine about this,' she lied.

'Really?'

She nodded. 'It's about time I finally made it down the aisle, don't you think?'

'He'll take care of you.' He squeezed her hand. 'You'll take care of each other. You know your mother was the love of my life...'

Hannah felt a heart-squeezing clutch of sadness. 'Yes, Dad.'

'She didn't love me when we got married. She was pregnant, and I persuaded her... What I'm trying to say is that it's possible to grow to love someone. She did.'

Incredibly moved by his confidences, she nodded, her throat aching with unshed tears. There was no point telling him the cases were totally dissimilar. Her father had loved the woman he had married, whereas Hannah was marrying a man who despised her.

A man who had saved her life.

Any moment she would wake up.

But it wasn't a dream. However surreal it felt, she really was standing there with her hand on her father's arm, about to walk down the aisle to be married to a stranger.

'Ready?' her father asked.

She struggled to relearn the forgotten skill of smiling for his benefit and nodded. Ahead of her the elegant Raini spoke to someone outside Hannah's line of vision and the big doors swung open.

Hannah had anticipated more of the same magnificence she had encountered so far, but she had the impression of a space that was relatively small, almost intimate...peaceful. The tranquillity was a dramatic contrast to the emotional storm that raged just below her calm surface.

If you discounted the priest and choir there were only four people present: two robed rulers in the pews, and the two men who stood waiting, one tall and fair, the other…the other tall and very dark. She closed her eyes and willed herself to relax, to breathe, to do this… She opened them again and smiled at her father. He felt bad enough about this without her falling apart.

'Nervous?'

Kamel glanced at his best man. 'No.' Resigned would be a more accurate description of his mindset. There had only ever been one woman he had imagined walking down the aisle towards him and he had watched her make that walk to someone else. He would never forget the expression on her face—she had been incandescent with joy. Yet now when he did think of it he found another face superimposing itself over Amira's. A face framed by blonde hair.

'I suppose you could call this a version of a shotgun wedding,' the other man mused, glancing at the two royal personages who occupied the empty front pews. 'She's not…?'

He tried to imagine those blue eyes soft as she held a child. 'No, she is not.'

'There's going to be a hell of a lot of pressure

for you to change that. I hope she knows what she's letting herself in for.'

'Did you?' Kamel countered, genuinely curious.

'No, but then I didn't marry the heir apparent...which is maybe just as well. Raini and I have decided not to go for another round of IVF. It's been eight years now and there has to be a cut-off point. There is a limit to how many times she can put herself through this.'

Kamel clasped the other man's shoulder. 'Sorry.'

The word had never sounded less adequate. Kamel never lost sight of the fact that life was unfair, but if he had this would have reminded him. The world was filled with children who were unloved and unwanted and here were two people who had all the love in the world to give a child and it wasn't going to happen for them.

One of life's cruelties.

'Thanks.' Steven looked towards a security guy who nodded and spoke into his earpiece. 'Looks like she's arrived on time. You're a lucky man.'

Kamel glanced at Steven and followed the

direction of his gaze. The breath caught in his throat. Bedraggled, she had been a beautiful woman, but this tall, slender creature was a dream vision in white—hair falling like a golden cloud down her back, the diamonds glittering on her lacy veil fading beside the brilliance of her wide blue eyes.

'That remains to be seen.'

Kamel's murmured comment drew a quizzical look from his best man but no response that could be heard above the strains of 'Ave Maria' sung by the choir as the bride on her father's arm, preceded by her matron of honour, began her progression.

A weird sense of calm settled on Hannah as she stood facing her bridegroom. It did not cross her mind until afterwards that the whole thing resembled an out-of-body experience: she was floating somewhere above the heads of the people gathered to witness this parody, watching herself give her responses in a voice that didn't even hold a tremor.

The tremor came at the end when they were pronounced man and wife and Kamel looked directly at her for the first time. His dark eyes held hers as he brushed a fold of gossamer lace from her cheek and stared down at her with a soul-stripping intensity.

In her emotionally heightened state she had no idea who leaned in to whom; Hannah just knew she experienced the weirdest sensation, as though she were being pulled by an invisible thread towards him.

Her eyes were wide open as he covered her lips with his, then as the warm pressure deepened her eyelids lowered and her lips parted without any coercion and she kissed him back.

It was Kamel who broke the contact. Without it, her head was no longer filled with the taste, the texture and the smell of him, and reality came flooding back with a vengeance. She'd just kissed her husband and she'd enjoyed it—more than a little. That was wrong, so *very* wrong on every level. It was as if he had flicked a switch she didn't know she had. She shivered, unable to control the fresh wave of heat that washed over her skin.

He took her hand and raised it to his lips,

watching the rapt glow of sensual invitation in her velvet eyes be replaced by something close to panic. He was not shocked but he was surprised by the strength of the physical response she had shown.

'Smile. You're the radiant bride, *ma belle*,' he warned.

Hannah smiled until her jaw ached. She smiled all the way through the formality of signatures, and all she could think about was that kiss. The memory felt like a hot prickle under her skin. For the first time in her life she understood the power of sex and how a person could forget who they were under the influence of that particular drug.

She was kissed on both cheeks by the leaders of two countries, and then rather more robustly by her father, who held her hand tightly.

'You know that I am always there for you, Hannah.'

'I know, Dad. I'm fine.' She blinked away emotional tears but couldn't dislodge the massive lump in her throat.

'I will take care of her, Charles.'

His sincerity made her teeth ache. You couldn't trust a man who could lie so well, not that Hannah had any intention of trusting him. Aware that her father was watching, she let it lie when Kamel took her hand in his, not snatching it away until they were out of sight.

His only reaction was a sardonic smirk.

It took ten minutes after the farewells for them to walk back to his private apartments. His bride didn't say a word the whole time.

It was hard not to contrast the brittle ice queen beside him with the woman whose soft warm lips he had tasted. That small taste, the heat that had flared between them, shocking with its intensity and urgency, had left him curious, and eager to repeat the experience.

He was lusting after his bride. Well, life was full of surprises and not all of them were bad. The situation suited a man who had a very pragmatic approach to sex.

The room they stood in was on the same grand scale as all the others. This one apparently connected two bedrooms, if she had understood him correctly. Her exhausted brain was filled with a low-level hum of confusion, and two images from the wedding kept flitting through her head—her father's tired, ill face and the predatory heat in Kamel's eyes when he claimed his kiss.

'Has it occurred to you that this marriage might not be something to be endured...but enjoyed?'

Hannah's fingers slipped off the door handle. She turned around, her back against the wooden panels. He was standing too close...much too close. She struggled to draw in air as her body stirred, responding to the slumberous, sensual provocation shining in his dark eyes.

'The only thing I want to enjoy tonight is some privacy.'

'That is not what you would enjoy.'

She threw up her hands in a gesture of exasperated defeat. 'Fine! So I find you attractive. Is that what you want to hear?' She angled a scornful glance up at his lean dark face. 'I find any number of men attractive, but I don't sleep with them all.'

Make that none.

'You're discerning. I like that in you.'

'You may be good to look at but your ego is a massive turn-off.'

'I could work on it. You would teach me.'

Big, predatory, and sinfully sexy—she was willing to bet that that were quite a few things he could teach her! Her stomach tightened in self-disgust. Shocked by the thought that had insinuated itself into her head, she tilted her chin, channelling all the ice princess she could muster, and retorted haughtily, 'I'm not into casual sex or tutoring.'

'We're married, *ma belle*. That is not *casual*... and I do not need instruction.'

Hannah's eyes went to the ring on her finger. It felt heavy. She felt...*consumed*. She frowned at the word that formed in her head. Consumed by feelings, a need. She gave her head a tiny shake. It was dangerous to imagine something that was not there. She blamed the bottle of champagne that Raini had cracked open in the limo. Had she had one or two glasses? Regardless of her alcohol consumption, the only thing she needed was sleep.

He laid a hand on the door beside her head and leaned into her. 'Well, if you change your mind you know where I am.' His eyes not leaving hers, he tipped his head at the door next to her own. 'And for the record I'm fine with...just sex. I will not feel used or cheap in the morning.'

His throaty, mocking laugh was the last straw.

Her blue eyes narrowed and her chin lifted to a combative angle. She could actually feel something inside her snapping as she reached up and pulled his face down until she could reach his lips. In the instant before she covered his mouth with hers she saw his expression change—saw the mockery vanish and the dark, dangerous glow slide into his heavy-lidded eyes.

In the tiny corner of her mind that was still sane Hannah knew she was doing something incredibly stupid, but it was too late to pull back, and then he was kissing her back with a sensual skill that made her sleep-deprived brain shut down—she just clung on for the ride.

Kamel was a man who was rarely surprised—but Hannah had surprised him twice already.

First when she kissed him, and second when lust slammed through his body.

Had he ever wanted a woman this badly?

Then he identified the flavour of her kiss. As he pulled away she clung like a limpet, a very soft, warm, inviting limpet, but he gritted his teeth. He knew that if he let it go on a moment longer he wouldn't be able to stop. And when he made love to his wife he wanted her not just willing but awake and sober!

He studied her flushed face, the bright, almost febrile glitter in her eyes. He had seen the same look in the eyes of a friend who, after pulling three consecutive all-nighters before an exam, had fallen asleep halfway through the actual exam. Hannah was seriously sleep deprived, and more than a bit tipsy.

As a rule he thought it was nice if the person you were making love to stayed conscious. He gave a self-mocking smile. Being noble was really overrated—no wonder it had fallen out of fashion.

'You've been drinking.'

She blinked at the accusation, then insisted loudly, 'I'm not drunk!'

The pout she gave him almost broke his resolve. 'We won't argue the point,' he said wearily. 'I think we should sleep on this. Goodnight, Hannah.'

And he walked away and left her standing there feeling like…like…like a woman who'd just made a pass at her own husband and got knocked back. So not only did she now feel cheap, she felt unattractive. Rejected by two fiancés, and now a husband, but she couldn't summon the energy to care as, with a sigh, she fell backwards fully clothed onto the bed, closed her eyes and was immediately asleep.

CHAPTER SIX

TOO PROUD TO ask for help, Hannah was lost. She finally located Kamel in the fourth room she tried—one that opened off a square, windowless hallway that might have been dark but for the daylight that filtered through the blue glass of the dome high above.

Like the ones before it, this room was massive and imposing, and also came complete with a built-in echo, and her heels were particularly noisy on the inlaid floor. But Kamel didn't look up. The hawk on its perch followed her with its dark eyes while her master continued to stare at the screen of his mobile phone with a frown of concentration that drew his dark brows into a straight line above his aquiline nose.

Choosing not to acknowledge the strange achy feeling in the pit of her stomach, she walked up to the desk and cleared her throat.

When his dark head didn't lift she felt her temper fizz and embraced the feeling. If he wanted to be awkward, fine. She could do awkward. She felt damned awkward after last night.

'Is this your doing?' Realising that her posture, with her arms folded tightly across her stomach, might be construed as protective, she dropped them to her sides.

Kamel stopped scrolling through his emails, looked up from his phone and smiled. 'Good morning, dear wife.'

Kamel did not feel it was a particularly good morning and it had been a very bad night. He felt tired, and more frustrated than any man should be after his wedding night. A cold shower, a long run and he had regained a little perspective this morning. But then she walked in the room and just the scent of her perfume... He wanted her here and now. *The difference between want and need* was important to Kamel. He had not allowed himself to *need* a woman since Amira.

He *needed* sex, not Hannah. And the sex would be good—his icy bride turned out to have more fire in her than any woman he had ever met. But afterwards he would feel as he always did—the escape from the tight knot of brutal loneliness in his chest was only ever temporary.

Hannah's lips tightened at the mockery but she did not react to it; instead she simply arched a feathery brow. *'Well?'*

'I feel as though I am walking into this conversation midway through. Coffee?' He lifted the pot on the desk beside him and topped up his half-filled cup and allowed his gaze to drift over her face. 'Hangover?'

'No,' she lied. The delicious aroma drifted her way, making her mouth water. She felt shivery as she struggled to tear her eyes off his long brown fingers. 'I don't want coffee.'

'So can I help you with something?'

She emitted a soft hissing sound of annoyance. Without looking back, she pointed to the open doorway where a suited figure stood, complete with enigmatic expression and concealed weapon. 'Did you arrange for him to follow me?'

Kamel stood up from the desk and walked past her towards the open door. Nodding to the man standing outside, he closed it with a soft thud and turned back to Hannah, though his attention appeared to be on the lie of his narrow silk tie that lay in a flash of subdued colour against his white shirt. The jacket that matched the dove-grey trousers was draped across the back of the chair.

'For heaven's sake, you look ridiculously perfect.'

Her delivery lacked the scornful punch she had intended, possibly because the comment was no exaggeration. The pale grey trousers that matched the jacket were clearly bespoke and could have been cut to disguise a multitude of sins if he'd had any, but there was no escaping the fact that physically at least he was flawless.

He raised his brows and she felt her cheeks colour. 'I despise men who spend more time looking in the mirror than I do.'

'Rather a sexist thing to say,' he remarked, his tone mildly amused and his eyes uncomfortably observant. 'But each to his own. I'm sorry I don't measure up to your unwashed grunge ideal.'

Having dug herself a hole, she let the subject drop. He could never fail to live up to any woman's ideal, on a purely eye-candy level, of course. 'I do not require a bodyguard.'

'No, obviously not.'

Her pleased smile at a battle so easily won had barely formed when his next words made it vanish.

'You will require a team of them.'

'That's ludicrous!' she contended furiously.

The amusement in his manner vanished as he countered, 'It's necessary, so I suggest you stop acting like a diva and accept it.'

'I refuse.'

His glance slid from her flashing eyes to her heaving bosom, lingering there long enough to bring her hand to her throat. 'Refuse all you like, it won't alter anything. I appreciate this is an adjustment and I'll make allowances.'

That was big of him. 'Allowances! This is a palace! How do I adjust to that?'

'I have been to Brent Hall and it is hardly a council flat,' he retorted, thinking of the portrait that hung above the fireplace in the drawing room. Had Hannah Latimer ever possessed the dreamy innocence that shone in the eyes of her portrait, or had the artist been keen to flatter the man who was paying him?

She opened her mouth to retort and then his comment sank in. 'You've been to my home?'

He tipped his head. 'I stood in for my uncle on one social occasion, actually two. I predict you will adjust to your change in status. After all, you have played the pampered princess all your life. The only difference now is you have an actual title, and, of course, me.'

'I'm trying to forget.'

'Not the best idea.'

Despite the monotone delivery, she heard the warning and she didn't like it, or him.

Kamel gave a tolerant nod and picked up a pen from the desk. 'It is a fact of life. You will not leave this building without a security presence.'

'I wasn't outside the building. He was waiting outside my bedroom. What harm was I likely to come to there?'

'Oh, so your concern is for your privacy.'

'Well, yes. Obviously.' The idea of living like a bird in a golden cage did not hold any appeal. She'd given up her freedom but there had to be boundaries. Where were your boundaries last night, Hannah?

'We will be private enough, I promise you.'

The seductive promise in his voice sent a beat of white-hot excitement whipping through her body. As it ebbed she was consumed by hot-cheeked embarrassment.

'You blush very easily.'

She slung him a belligerent glare. 'I'm not used to the heat.' The desert heat she might grow accustomed to, but being around a man who could make her feel…feel…she gave a tiny gusty sigh as she sought for a word to describe how he made her feel, and it came—*hungry*! That was something she would never get used to. She just hoped it would pass quickly like a twenty-four-hour bug.

'So this is an example of how my life will not change?' she charged shrilly. 'I left one cell with a guard outside for another.'

'But the facilities and décor are much better,' he came back smoothly.

The languid smile that tugged the corner of his mouth upwards did not improve her mood. Neither did looking at his mouth. It was a struggle not to lift a hand to her own tingling lips. So far he hadn't mentioned the kiss. Had he forgotten?

She wished she had, but her memory loss only lasted until she had stood under a shower and then the whole mortifying scene came rushing back.

'This isn't a joke.'

The shriller she got, the calmer he became. 'Neither is it a subject for screaming and shouting and stamping your little foot.'

He glanced down at the part of her under discussion. She had very nice ankles but she had even nicer calves. He found his eyes drawn to the silky smooth contours and higher… The skirt of the dress she wore, a silky blue thing, sleeveless and cinched in at the waist with a narrow plaited tan belt, ended just above the knee. The entire image was cool, perfectly groomed… regal.

He refused to allow the image of his hands sliding under the fabric up and over the smooth curves—but the suggestion had been enough to send a streak of heat through his body where it coalesced into a heavy ache in his groin. He could have woken up this morning in her arms. Even while he had called himself a fool during the long wakeful night, he had known it was the right decision.

'I did not stamp my foot,' Hannah retorted and immediately wanted to do just that.

'But you have a tendency to turn everything into a drama, angel.'

Her brows hit her smooth hairline exposed by the severe hairstyle she had adopted that morning. The woman who had looked back at her from the mirror after she had speared the last hair grip into the smooth coil did not even look like a distant relative of the woman with the flushed face, feverishly bright eyes and swollen lips she had glimpsed in the mirror last night before she had fallen onto the bed fully dressed.

'If *this* isn't a drama, what is?'

'I appreciate this is not easy, but we are *both* living with the consequences of your actions.'

She threw up her hands and didn't even register the discomfort as one of the pearl studs she wore went flying across the room. She sighed heavily and asked, 'How many times a day are you going to remind me it's all my fault?'

'It depends on how many times you irritate me.' Kamel left his desk and walked to the spot where the pearl had landed beside the window.

'My breathing irritates you,' she said.

He elevated a dark brow. 'Not if you do it quietly.' He half closed his eyes, imagining hearing her breath quicken as he moved in and out of her body.

Hannah was not breathing quietly now. The closer he got, the louder her breathing became, then she stopped altogether. 'You are...' The trapped air left her lungs in one soft, sibilant sigh as he stopped just in front of her, close enough for her to feel the heat from his body.

'Have you ever heard of personal space?' she asked, tilting back her head to meet his challenging dark stare as she fought an increasingly strong impulse to step back. Her cool vanished into shrill panic as he leaned in towards her. 'What are you doing?'

More to the point, what was she doing?

She had tried so hard *not* to look at his mouth,

not to think of that kiss, it became inevitable that she was now staring and not in a casual way at his mouth and the only thing she could think about was that kiss—the firm texture of his lips, the heat of his mouth, the moist...

'You lost this.'

It took a few seconds to bring into focus the stud he held between his thumb and forefinger. When she realised what he was holding her hand went jerkily to her ear...the wrong one.

'No, this one.' He touched her ear lobe, catching it for a moment between his thumb and forefinger before letting it drop away. 'Pretty.' Her head jerked to one side, causing a fresh stab of pain to slide like a knife through her skull. How long before the headache tablets she had swallowed kicked in?

The strength of her physical response to the light contact sent a stab of alarm through Hannah. She swayed slightly and shifted her position, taking a step back. It no longer seemed so important to stand her ground. Live to fight another day—wasn't that what they said about those who ran away?

'Thank you,' she breathed, holding out her hand as she focused on his left shoulder.

He ignored the hand and leaned in closer. *Help,* she thought, her smile little more now than a scared fixed grimace painted on. Her nostrils quivered in reaction to the warm scent of his body, his nearness. She could feel the heat of his body through his clothes and hers…imagine how hot his skin would feel without…

And she did imagine; her core temperature immediately jumped by several painful degrees as she stood there in an agony of shame and arousal while he placed a thumb under her chin to angle her face up to him.

She'd decided that the only plus point in being married to a man she loathed was that she would never again suffer the pain and humiliation of rejection. She wouldn't care. A lovely theory, but hard to cling to when every cell in her body craved his touch. She had never felt this way before.

She bit her lip, fearing that if she set free the ironic laugh locked in her throat there would be a chain reaction—she would lose it and she couldn't do that. Pretty much all she had left was her pride.

Listen to yourself, Hannah, mocked the voice in her head. Your pride is all you have left? Go down that road of self-pity and you'd pretty much end up being the spoilt shallow bitch your husband thinks you are.

Husband.

I'm married.

Third time lucky. Or as it happened, *unlucky*. She knew there were many women who would have envied her *unlucky* fate just as there had been girls at school who had envied her.

The influential clique who had decided to make the new girl's life a misery even before they'd discovered she was stupid. She'd thought so too until she'd been diagnosed as dyslexic at fourteen.

For a long time Hannah had wondered why—what had she done or said?—and then she'd had the opportunity to ask when she'd found herself sitting in a train compartment with one of her former tormentors, all grown up now.

Hannah had immediately got up to leave but

had paused by the door when the other woman had spoken.

'I'm sorry.'

And Hannah had asked the question that she had always wanted to ask.

'Why?'

The answer had been the same one her father had given her when she had sobbed, 'What have I done? What's wrong with me?'

'It's got nothing to do with you, Hannah. They do it because they can. I could move you to another school, sweetheart, but what happens if the same thing happens there? You can't carry on running away. The way to cope with bullies is not to react. Don't let them see they get to you.'

The strategy had worked perhaps too well because, not only had her cool mask put off the bullies, but potential friends too, except for Sal.

What would Sal say? She closed off that line of thought, but not before she experienced a wave of deep sadness. She didn't share secrets with Sal any more; she had lost her best friend the day she had found her in bed with her fiancé. It was to have been her wedding day.

And now here she was, a married woman. Kamel's touch was deft, almost clinical, but there was nothing clinical about the shimmies of sensation that zigzagged through her body as his fingers brushed her ear lobe.

Hannah breathed again when he straightened up, keeping her expression as neutral as his.

'Thank you,' she murmured distantly. 'Could you tell me where the kitchen is?'

He looked surprised by the question. 'I haven't the faintest idea.'

'You don't know where your own kitchen is?'

Kamel, who still looked bemused, ignored her question. 'Why were you going to the kitchen?' he persisted. 'If you want a tour of the place the housekeeper will…'

'I didn't want a tour. I wanted breakfast.' She had eaten nothing the previous evening. Unfortunately she had not shown similar restraint when it came to the champagne.

'Why didn't you ring for something?'

'Do you really not know where your kitchen is?'

He arched a sardonic brow. 'And am I meant

to believe you do? That you are a regular visitor to the kitchens at Brent Hall?' It was not an area he had seen on the occasion he had been a guest at Charles Latimer's country estate, a vast Elizabethan manor with a full complement of staff. The daughter of the house had not been home at the time but her presence had been very much felt.

There was barely a polished surface in the place that did not have a framed photo of her and her accomplishments through the years—playing the violin, riding a horse, looking athletic with a tennis racket, looking academic in a gown and mortar board.

And looking beautiful in the portrait in the drawing room over the fireplace.

'He really caught her,' the proud father had said when he'd found Kamel looking at it.

His sarcastic drawl set her teeth on edge. 'I left home at eighteen.'

And by then Hannah had been a very good cook, thanks to her father's chef at Brent Hall. Sarah Curtis had an impressive professional pedigree, she had worked in top kitchens around Europe and she had a daughter who had no interest in food or cooking. When she'd realised that Hannah did, she'd encouraged that interest.

For Hannah the kitchen was a happy place, the place her father came and sat in the evenings, where he shed his jacket and his formality. She had not realised then why…now she did.

'Yes, I can imagine the hardship of picking out an outfit and booking a table every night must have been difficult. What taxing subject did you study?'

'Classics,' she snapped.

'So you spent a happy three years learning something incredibly useful.'

'Four actually. I needed extra time because I'm dyslexic.'

'You have dyslexia?'

'Which doesn't mean I'm stupid.'

It was a taunt she had obviously heard before, and taunts left scars. Kamel experienced a swift surge of anger as he thought of the people responsible for creating this defensive reflex. In his opinion it was them, not Hannah, who could be accused of stupidity...ignorance...cruelty.

Kamel was looking at her oddly. The silence stretched. Was he worried their child might inherit her condition? He might be right, but at least she'd know what signs to look for—he or she wouldn't have to wait until they were a teenager before they had a diagnosis.

'You have dyslexia and you got a degree in Classics?' Now that was something that required serious determination.

'Not a first, but I can make a cup of tea and toast a slice of bread, and at least I don't judge people I don't know...' She stopped and thought, Why am I playing it down? 'I got an upper second and actually I'm a good cook—*very* good.' She'd be even better if she had accepted the internship at the restaurant that Sarah had wangled for her: awful hours, menial repetitive tasks and the chance to work under a three-star Michelin chef.

For once she hadn't been able to coax her father around to her way of thinking—he had exploded when he'd learnt of the plan. It hadn't just been to please him that instead she had accepted the prestigious university place she had been offered; it had been because she had realised that the contentious issue of her career had become a major issue between her father and his cook.

His mistress.

The smile that hitched one corner of Kamel's mouth upwards did not touch his eyes; they remained thoughtful, almost wary. 'I have married a clever woman and a domestic goddess. Lucky me.'

Her jaw tightened at what she perceived as sarcasm.

'Lucky me,' he repeated, seeing her in the wedding dress, her face clustered with damp curls, her lips looking pink and bruised, her passion-glazed eyes heavy and deep blue, not cold, but hot. He rubbed his thumb absently against his palm, mimicking the action when he had stroked her cheek, feeling the invisible fuzz of invisible downy hair on the soft surface.

The contrast with the cold, classy woman before him could not have been more dramatic; they were both beautiful but the woman last night had been sexy, sinfully hot, available—but married. He didn't sleep with drunk women; the choice was normally an end-of-story shrug, not hours of seething frustration while he wrestled his passion into submission, cursing his black and white sense of honour.

The same honour that had made him push Amira into Hakim's arms.

He was either a saint or an idiot!

Hannah gave a mental shrug and turned a slender shoulder, telling herself that it didn't matter what he thought of her...she still wanted to hit him.

Or kiss him.

Dusting an invisible speck off her silk dress, she gave a faint smile and thought about slapping that expression of smug superiority off his hateful face.

'Relax, we leave at twelve-thirty.'

Relax, no. But this was the best news she had had in several nightmare days.

'Where are you off to?' She didn't care but it seemed polite to ask.

'*We.*'

Her expression froze. 'We? What are you talking about? There is no we!'

'Please do not treat me to another bout of your histrionics. Behind closed doors there is no we.' Lips twisted into a sardonic smile, he sat on the edge of the desk. 'But in public we are a loving couple and you will show me respect.'

'When you stop lying to me. You said we would not have to live together.'

'You didn't really believe that. I said what you wanted to hear. It seemed the kindest thing at the time.'

She let out a snort of sheer disbelief—was this man for real? 'Perhaps I should thank you for kindly lying through your teeth.'

He glanced at the watch on his wrist, exposing the fine dark hairs on his arm as he flicked his cuff. 'Quite clearly we have things to discuss,' he conceded.

Hannah, who was breathing hard, flashed a bitter smile. 'Discuss' implied reasonable and flexible. It implied listening. *You think?*'

He refused to recognise the irony in her voice. 'Yes, I do think.'

'You are giving me a time slot?' She was married to a man she was expected to make an appointment to talk to? Now that really brought home how awful this entire situation was. She had walked into it with her eyes wide open and her brain in denial. The fact was that deep down she had never stopped being a person who believed in happy ever after, who believed that everything happened for a reason.

A spasm of irritation crossed his lean, hard features.

She shook her head and gave a laugh of sheer disbelief. 'Or should that be granting me an audience?' she wondered, letting her head tip forward as she performed a mocking curtsey.

The childish reaction made his jaw clench.

'You're used to people dropping everything when you require attention. But I've got a newsflash…' He let the sentence hang, but the languid contempt in his voice made it easy to fill in the blanks as he glanced down at the stack of papers spread out on the inlaid table.

It wasn't that she wanted to be important to him, but a little empathy—she'd have settled for civility—would have made him human. Instead he intended to map out just how insignificant she was in the scheme of things from the outset. Did he really think she didn't know she was on the bottom rung of his priorities?

Hannah could feel the defensive ice forming on her features. 'Sorry,' she said coldly. 'I'm still living in a world where people have marriages based on mutual respect, not mutual contempt! It was unrealistic of me, and it won't happen again,' she promised. 'I won't disturb you any longer. Have your people talk to my people and...' The ice chips left her voice as it quivered... My people. I have no people. The total isolation of her position hit home for the first time.

She squeezed her eyes shut.

'I need an hour.'

She opened her eyes and found he was looking right at her. Her stomach immediately went into a dive.

'I could postpone this but I assumed you would prefer to arrive early at Brent.'

Her eyes flew wide. 'Brent!' She gave a shaky smile. 'You're taking me home?'

'This is your home.'

Swallowing the hurt and annoyed with herself for leaping to conclusions, she lifted her chin and stared at him coldly. 'This will never be my home.'

'That, *ma belle*, is up to you. But your father wanted to hold a wedding party for us, and for your friends. I think it would only be polite for us to be there. I will have some breakfast sent up to your room.'

Jaw clenched at the dismissal, Hannah left the room with her head held high.

CHAPTER SEVEN

HER FATHER WAS there to greet them at the private airstrip where they landed, and Hannah was relieved he looked better than the previous day, almost his old self. She was sandwiched between the two men in the back seat of the limo and by the time they arrived at Brent Hall the effort of maintaining a reassuring pretence for her father's sake had taken its toll, her persistent nagging headache showing signs of becoming a full-blown migraine.

'I think I might go to my room, unless you want me to help.' There was evidence of the preparations for tonight everywhere.

'No, you have a rest. Good idea. Tonight is all under control. I got a new firm in and they seem excellent—they're doing the lot. I have a few ideas I want to run past your husband.' He glanced towards Kamel and joked, 'Not much point having a financial genius in the family if you don't make use of him, is there? I'm sure he'll even write your thank-you letters.'

Hannah laughed and her father winked conspiratorially at her. 'A family joke.'

And one that was at his daughter's expense, thought Kamel, who had seen the flinch before the smile. How many times, he wondered, had she been on the receiving end of such jokes? For a man who cared deeply for his daughter, Charles Latimer seemed remarkably blind to her sensitivity.

'I am aware of Hannah's dyslexia. Is that the family joke?'

'She told you?' Hannah's father looked startled.

'She did. But even if she hadn't I would have noticed how uncomfortable the family *joke* made her.'

Hannah's father looked horrified by the suggestion. 'It's just that some of her mistakes have been so...' His stammering explanation ground to a halt in the face of his new son-in-law's fixed, unsmiling stare. 'Hannah has a great sense of humour.'

'I don't.'

Instead of heading for her room, Hannah made her way down to the kitchens. But finding the place had been taken over by outside caterers, she made her way to Sarah's private flat.

The cook was delighted to see her. So was Olive, the dog sitting in her basket, surrounded by her puppies, who licked Hannah's hand and wagged her stumpy little tail.

Without being asked, Sarah produced some painkillers along with the coffee and cakes. 'Now, tell me all about it.'

Hannah did—or at least the approved version. She stayed half an hour before she got up to leave.

'Where are you going?' Sarah called after her.

'To my room. I need to get ready.' She pulled a face.

'Not that way, Hannah.' Sarah laughed. 'You can't sleep in your old bedroom. You're a married woman now.'

'Oh, God, I forgot!' Hannah groaned.

If the cook thought this was an odd thing to say she didn't let on. Instead she enthused about the complete refurbishment of the guest suite that Hannah was to stay in. 'Mind you, if you're used to palaces...'

'I'm not used to palaces. I'll never be used to palaces. I hate them and I hate him!' Then it all came tumbling out—the whole story.

'I knew something was wrong,' Sarah said as she piled sugar in a cup of tea and made Hannah drink it. 'I don't know what to say, Hannah. I really don't.'

'There's nothing to say. I'm sorry I dumped on you like this.'

'Heavens, girl, that's what I'm here for. You know I've always thought of you as my second daughter.'

'I wish I was,' Hannah replied fiercely, envying Eve her mother. 'Dad thinks I'm all right with it. You won't tell him, will you? I worry so much that the stress will…' She didn't have to explain her worries to Sarah, who knew about the heart attack. She'd been with Hannah when she'd got the call and had travelled with her to the hospital.

Having extracted a firm promise that Sarah would not reveal how unhappy she was, Hannah made her way to the guest room and discovered that Sarah had not exaggerated about the makeover.

She explored the luxurious bedroom. An opulent silk curtained four-poster bed occupied one end of the room. She quickly looked away, but not before several illicit images slipped through her mental block. Her stomach was still flipping lazily as she focused on the opposite end of the room where a bathtub deep enough to swim in sat on a raised dais.

Behind it there were two doors. One opened, she discovered, into a massive wet room— she pressed one of the buttons on a glass control panel that would have looked at home in a space station and the room was filled with the sounds of the ocean. Unable to locate a button that turned it off, she closed the door and pushed open the other door. The lights inside automatically lit up, revealing a space that was the size of her entire flat, lined with hanging space, mirrors and shelves.

It was not a full wardrobe, but neither was it empty. The selection of clothes and shoes that were hung and neatly folded were her own. Shoes, bags, underclothes—there was something for every occasion, including an obvious choice for this evening where all eyes would be on her. She pushed away the thought of the evening ahead and lifted a silk shirt to her face. Feeling the sharp prick of tears behind her eyelids, she blinked them back.

After the last few days Hannah had imagined that nothing could shock her ever again. But when she opened the large velvet box on the dressing table and looked at the contents displayed on the silk lining, she knew that she had been wrong!

Kamel glanced at the closed door, then at his watch. He was expecting her to be late and he was expecting her to be hostile; she was neither. At seven on the dot the door opened and his wife stepped into the room.

Kamel struggled to contain his gasp. He had seen her at her worst and that had been beautiful. At her best she was simply breathtaking. The satin gown she wore with such queenly confidence left one shoulder bare, Grecian style. The bodice cut snugly across her breasts, continued in a body-hugging column to the knee where it flared out, sweeping the ground. Her skin against the black glowed with a pearly opalescence.

The silence stretched and Hannah fought the absurd urge to curtsey. What was she meant to do—ask for marks out of ten?

Anxiety gnawed her stomach lining and tension tied the muscles in her shoulders but her expression was serene as she took a step towards him and fought the ridiculous urge to ask for his approval. 'Am I late?'

'You are not wearing the diamonds,' he said, noticing the absence of the jewels he had had removed from the vault that morning.

'I'm a "less is more" kind of girl.' She could not explain even to herself her reluctance to wear the jewels.

He arched a sardonic brow. 'And I'm an "if you have it flaunt it" sort of guy.'

'All right, I'll put them on,' she agreed without good grace before sweeping from the room. 'Satisfied now?' she asked when she returned a short while later wearing the jewellery. On the plus side, nobody would be looking at her now—they'd be staring at the king's ransom she wore.

Hannah watched the lift doors opening and felt her stomach go into a steep dive. She did not question the instinct that warned her not to be in an enclosed space with this man. She picked up her skirt in one hand. 'I'm fine with the stairs.'

'I'm not.'

Not anticipating the hand against the small of her back that propelled her forward, she tensed before retreating into a corner and standing there trying not to meet her own eyes in the mirrors that covered four walls of the lift.

She exited the lift a step ahead of him, almost falling out in the process.

'Relax.'

The advice drew a disbelieving laugh from the resentful recipient, who turned her head sharply and was reminded of the chandelier earrings she wore as they brushed her skin. '*Seriously?*'

The man had spent most of their flight giving her a last-minute crash course in how princesses were meant to behave. The consequences of her failing had not been spelt out, but had left her with the impression the political stability of a nation—or possibly even a continent—could be jeopardised by her saying the wrong word to the wrong person or using the wrong fork.

So no pressure, then!

'If I'd been listening to a word you said I'd be a gibbering wreck, but happily I've started as I mean to go on. I tuned you out.' She smiled at his expression, catching the flicker of shock in his eyes, and chalked a mental point in the air. Then, producing a brilliant smile, she laid a hand on his arm as they reached the double doors of the ballroom.

'I do know how to work a room, you know.'

Despite the assurance, she was actually glad to enter the room beside a figure who oozed authority. She'd been acting as a hostess for her

father for years, but it was a shock to find few
faces she recognised in the room.

Despite her initial misgivings, a glass of champagne later she was circulating, accepting con-
gratulations, smiling and doing a pretty good
job of lying through her clenched teeth. Until
she saw a familiar figure. She went to wave,
and then the man he was speaking to turned
his head.

She knew, of course, that her father and Rob
Preston still saw one another on a personal and
professional level, but her ex-fiancé had never
been invited to any event when she was present
previously.

Hannah moved across the room to where her
father stood chatting.

'Excuse me, can I borrow my father for one
minute?'

'What's wrong, Hannah?'

'Rob is here!'

'He is one of my oldest friends. You're married now, and I think it's time we drew a line
under what happened, if Rob is willing to forgive and forget.'

'I should too.' She took a deep breath. This was what happened when you put your pride before the truth. 'You're right, Dad. Fine,' she said, thinking that it was so not fine.

As the party progressed a few people began to drift outside into the courtyard, and Hannah joined them, having spent the evening avoiding Rob, who to her relief had shown no inclination to speak to her.

With the tree branches filled with white lights and the sound of laughter and music from inside drifting out through the open doors, it was a magical scene. Most people had sensibly avoided the damp grass and remained on the paved area around the pool, laughing and talking, all except a middle-aged couple who reappeared from amongst the trees. The woman's hair was mussed and her shoes were in her hand.

Hannah looked down at her own feet—they ached in the high heels that matched her gown. She wriggled her cramped toes, forcing blood back into the cramped extremities and wincing at the painful burn. What page on the princess handbook said you weren't allowed to take off your shoes and walk on the grass? It would be there along with anything else spontaneous and fun. The wistful ache in her throat grew heavier as she watched the man…maybe her husband… slide a shoe back onto the pretty woman's foot while she balanced precariously on the other. The woman tottered and her partner caught her. There was a lot of soft laughter and a brief kiss before they went back indoors.

Hannah was taking a last deep breath of fresh air and painting on a smile just as a figure emerged, his eyes scanning as if he was searching for something or someone. Her bodyguard stood out like a sore thumb, albeit one in black tie.

Hannah found herself moving backwards into the shadow of a tree. She realised she was holding her breath and closing her eyes like a child who wanted to disappear. She looked down at her hands clenched into tight fists and slowly unfurled them. The sight of the deep grooves her nails had cut into the flesh of her palm drew a fleeting frown of acknowledgement but didn't lessen her defiance.

The buzz lasted a few moments, but as the exhilaration of her small rebellion faded away she stared at her shoes sinking into the damp ground. Was this going to be her life in future? Ignoring 'don't walk on the grass' signs just to feel alive?

As rebellions went it was pathetic.

She was pathetic.

She took a deep breath and, taking her shoes off and holding them in one hand, she used the other to lift her skirt free of the damp grass as she straightened her slender shoulder. 'Man up, Hannah,' she muttered to herself as she moved towards the lights that filtered through the bank of trees.

'Hello, Hannah. I knew you wanted me to follow you.'

Hannah let out a soft yelp of shock and dropped both her shoes and skirt. The fabric trailed on the wet ground as she turned around.

The comment came from a man with a massive ego, a man who thought everything was about him.

The acknowledgement shocked Hannah more

than the fact Rob had followed her. Even after she had discovered his infidelities there had been a small, irrational corner of her brain that had made excuses for him.

There were no excuses, not for him and not for her either for being so damned gullible—for not seeing past the perfect manners, the practised smile and the thoughtful gifts. She'd seen little flashes of the real Rob and she'd chosen to ignore them and the growing unease she had felt. If she hadn't walked into Sal's room and found them…

She closed her eyes to blot out the mental image, and lifted her chin. She had been dreading this moment but now that it was here…how bad could it be? She'd spent two days in a prison cell. She could definitely cope with an awkward situation.

'Hello, Rob.' He'd been drinking heavily. She could smell it even before he stepped into the patch of moonlight and she was able to see his high colour and glazed eyes. Seeing Rob when she had thought he was the love of her life had always made her stomach quiver, but now it quivered with distaste.

'No, I didn't want you to follow me. I *really* didn't.'

He looked taken aback by her reaction. Clearly I'm not following the script he wrote, she thought. Drunk or not drunk, he was still a very handsome man, the premature silvered wings of hair giving him a distinguished look, along with the horn-rimmed glasses that she had been amazed to discover were plain glass, though they gave a superficial impression of intellect and sensitivity.

But then Rob always had been more about style than substance. Deep down Hannah had always known that, she had just chosen not to think about it. But for the first time now she was struck by a softness about him. Not just the thickness around the middle that regular sessions with a personal trainer could never quite eliminate, but in his features... Had he always looked that way or was it just the contrast? She had spent the last two days in the company of a man who made granite look soft.

An image of Kamel floated into her mind: his strong-boned aristocratic features, his mobile, sensual mouth.

'Just like old times. Remember the time we brought a bottle of champagne out here and—?'

Hannah stiffened and matched his hot stare with one of cold contempt. 'That wasn't me.'

He stopped, his eyes falling as his lips compressed in a petulant line. 'Oh! She never meant anything—'

Did he even remember who *she* was? The anger and bitterness was still there, and most of all the knowledge that she had been a total fool. But now she could see the black humour in it...in him.

He was a joke.

'And now you mean nothing to me.'

As he sensed her shift of attitude, sensed he had lost his power, his expression darkened. 'That's not true and we both know it.'

'Look, Rob, Dad wanted you to be here and that's fine. But you and I are never going to be friends. Let's settle for civil...?' She gave a sigh and felt relief. This was the moment she had been dreading—coming face to face with the man she had considered the love of her life only to discover he meant nothing.

Her relieved sigh became a sharp intake of alarm as Rob lumbered drunkenly towards her, forcing Hannah to retreat until her back hit the tree trunk. She winced as the bark grazed her back through the thin fabric of her gown.

'You were meant to be with me. We are soul mates… What went wrong, Hannah?'

A contemptuous laugh came from Hannah's lips. She was too angry at being manhandled to be afraid. 'Maybe all my friends—the ones you bedded after we were engaged?' She made the sarcastic suggestion without particular rancour. Rob was pathetic.

'I told you, they meant nothing. They were just cheap…' His lips curled. 'Not like you—you're pure and perfect. I was willing to wait for you. It would have been different after we were married. I would have given you everything.' He clasped a hand to his heart.

The dramatic gesture caused Hannah's discomfort to tip over into amusement. He looked so ridiculous.

His eyes narrowed at her laugh, then slid to the jewels that gleamed against the skin of her throat. 'But I wasn't enough for you, was I?'

She swallowed; the laugh had been a bad idea. 'I think I'd better go.'

'A love match, is it? Or should that be an oil deal?' He saw her look of shock and smiled. 'People talk, and I know a lot of people.'

On the receiving end of his fixed lascivious stare, she felt sick. 'Well, I'm not pure or perfect but I am extremely pis—'

Rob, in full florid flow, cut across her. 'A work of art,' he raved. 'Sheer perfection, my perfect queen, not his—he doesn't appreciate you like I would have. I'd have looked after you...the other women, they meant nothing to me,' he slurred. 'You must know that—you are the only woman I have ever loved.'

How did I ever think he was the man of my dreams? she wondered, feeling queasy as he planted a hand on the tree trunk beside her head and leaned in closer.

Struggling not to breathe in the fumes, she countered acidly, 'Well, you know, you can't miss what you've never had.'

Having followed the spiky imprints of her heels across the wet grass, Kamel took only a few minutes to locate the couple in the tree. He didn't pause. Unable to see them, he heard their voices as with a face like thunder he charged straight through a shrub.

This wasn't a moment to stop and consider, not a moment for subtlety. He'd bent over backwards to be reasonable but she wasn't a woman who responded to reasonable. Was she pushing boundaries, checking just how far she could push him? Or maybe she simply lacked any normal sense of propriety? This wasn't about jealousy. It was one thing to have a pragmatic approach to marriage, but she had not just crossed the line, she had obliterated it!

The couple came into his line of vision about the same moment that he mentally processed the interchange he had just heard. It was astonishing enough to stop him in his tracks.

'Well, he's welcome to you!'

Hannah struggled and failed to swallow a caustic retort to this petulant response. 'Well, the idea that I was your soul mate didn't last long, did it?'

'Bitch!' Rob snarled. 'You think you've landed on your feet now, but we all know what happens to people when they get in your husband's way...'

Hannah was shaken by the malice and ugly jealousy in his face. *Jealousy...!* She shook her head in disbelief. Perhaps he'd been acting the injured party so long he actually believed it.

The full realisation of just how lucky she had been hit home. She could have been married to him.

Her stomach gave a fresh shudder of disgust as she pulled in a breath, trying to surreptitiously ease away from him. As nice as it would have been to drop the icy dignity that had got her through that awful day, this wasn't the time and definitely not the place, she thought, to have the last word.

This could get ugly.

'They have a habit of disappearing.' He mimed

a slashing action across his throat. 'So watch yourself.'

The sinister comment drew a startled laugh from her. It was clearly not the reaction Rob had wanted, as his face darkened and he grabbed for her. Things happened with dizzying speed so that later when she thought about it Hannah couldn't recall the exact sequence of events.

Kamel surged forward but Hannah was quicker. Unable to escape, she ducked and her attacker's head hit the tree trunk with a dull thud.

Her attempt to slip under his arm was less successful, and by the time Kamel reached her the man, with blood streaming from a superficial head wound, had caught her arm and swung her back.

'Bitch!'

Hannah hit out blindly with her free hand and then quite suddenly she was free. Off balance, she fell and landed on her bottom on the wet grass. When she looked up Rob was standing with one hand twisted behind his back with Kamel whispering what she doubted were sweet nothings into the older man's ear, if the white-lipped fury stamped on his face was any indication.

Rob, who had blood seeping from a gash on his head, seemed to shrink before her eyes and started muttering excuses in full self-preservation mode.

'If I ever see you in the same postcode as my wife…if you so much as *look* in her direction…' Kamel leaned in closer, his nostrils flaring in distaste at the smell of booze and fear that enveloped the man like a cloud, and told him what would happen to him, sparing little detail.

Hannah struggled to her feet imagining the headlines. 'Don't hurt him!'

The plea caused Kamel's attention to swivel from the man he held to Hannah.

'Please?'

A muscle along his jaw clenched as he stared at her. Then, with a nod that caused two invisible figures to emerge from the trees, he stood aside and the trio walked away.

'Sure you don't want to go and hold his hand?'

'I wasn't protecting him. I was protecting you.' Why are you explaining yourself to him? she wondered. It's not as if he's going to believe you and it's not like you care what he thinks.

A look of scowling incredulity spread across his face. '*Me?* You are protecting *me*?' He had no idea why her caring about someone who was clearly an abusive loser bothered him so much, but it did.

Her eyes moved slowly up the long, lean length of his muscle-packed body. It was hard to imagine anyone who looked less like he needed looking after.

'The press could dub you something worse than The Heartbreaker Prince.' She paused and saw him absorb her comment. His anger still permeated the air around them but it simmered now where it had boiled before. 'Rob likes to play the victim. I can just see the headlines now…'

'I wasn't going to hit him, but if I had he wouldn't have been running to any scandal sheet,' he retorted, managing to sound every bit as sinister as Rob had implied he was. While Hannah believed Rob's comments were motivated by malice, there was no escaping the fact that she knew very little about the man she had married and what he was capable of.

Unwilling to release his image of her as a cold-hearted, unapproachable ice bitch, he asked, 'What the hell were you thinking of meeting him out here?'

What the hell had she been thinking about getting involved with him to begin with? The man had been mentally filed in his head as a victim. Stupid, but a victim, and now he turned out to be a… His fists clenched as he found himself wishing he had not shown restraint.

Temper fizzed through her body, sparking wrathful blue flames in her eyes. 'Are you implying that I arranged this? Rob followed me!'

'And I followed him.' It was an impulse that he had not checked even though it was a situation that had not required his personal intervention. In fact his abrupt departure had probably caused more speculation than Hannah's.

'Why? I thought you delegated all that sort of thing.'

'There are some things that a husband cannot delegate.' She might not be wife material but she was definitely mistress material. She might be the sort of woman he would normally cross the road to avoid, but there was no denying that physically she was perfect.

'So you thought it was your duty to rescue me.' She had about as much luck injecting amusement into her voice as she had escaping his dark, relentless stare. It was becoming harder to rationalise her response to his strong personal magnetism, or control the pulse-racing mixture of dread and excitement whenever he was close by.

'Little did I know you had it all under control.'

Her clenched teeth ached at the sarcasm. 'My hero riding to the rescue yet again.'

'I thought I was rescuing your...'

'Victim?'

He dragged his smouldering glance free of her cushiony soft lips and found himself staring at her heaving bosom. 'The man is...' He said a word that she didn't understand but it was not hard to get the drift. 'What is your ex doing at our wedding party?'

The accusation made her blink. 'The word

party suggests celebration. Tonight has felt more like a punishment. And yes, we all know this is my fault, though I have to tell you that line is getting a bit boring. I'm willing to take my medicine and make nice and pretend you're almost as marvellous as you think you are, but if this marriage is going to last, and I'm talking beyond the next few seconds, it won't be on a speak-when-you're-spoken-to, walk-two-steps-behind-me way. I am *not* willing to be a doormat!'

She released a shuddering sigh and warmed to her theme. 'So from now on I expect to be treated with some damned respect, and not just in public!' Oh, God! Overwhelmed with a mixture of horror and exhilaration, she could not recall losing control of herself quite so completely in her life. Hannah brought her lashes down in a protective veil as she gulped in several shallow breaths while her heart rate continued to race.

The ice queen is dead! Long live the princess of passion! His mental headline tugged the corners of his mouth upwards, but the curve flattened out as he felt his body stir lustfully. It wasn't the physical response that bothered him; it was the strength of it and the fact it kept intruding.

Mentally and physically, discipline and order were important to Kamel. He had never made a conscious decision to compartmentalise the disparate aspects of his life, but he took the ability for granted and it enabled him to combine the role he had unexpectedly inherited and any sort of personal life.

It had not crossed his mind that being married would lead to any overlap. Tonight came under the heading of duty, with a capital D. Such occasions were more than useful, they were essential, and he *definitely* shouldn't be thinking about how she'd look naked, and how soft and inviting her mouth was. Had she just said what he thought she had? He clenched his teeth and struggled to regroup his thoughts. Focus, Kamel—but not on her mouth.

'Would I be right in thinking that was an...' he spoke slowly, winged brows drawn into a straight line, and shaking his head slightly as though the concept he was about to voice was just so off the planet as to be unreal '...*ulti-matum?*'

Hannah didn't pause to analyse the weirdness in his voice. If he wanted to call it that it was fine by her! Like an angry curtain, the protective veil of her lashes lifted, but her militant response was delayed as their glances connected and the subsequent sensual jolt caused her brain to stall.

'I if...I...?'

The nerve endings in her brain might have stopped sending messages, but during that long, nerve-shredding pause those elsewhere had stepped up to fill the vacuum. She could almost feel the blood racing through her veins—it felt dark and hot like the ache low in her pelvis. She snatched a breath, let it out in a quivering sigh, and lifted her chin.

'Yes, it is, and,' she added, wagging her finger as she took a squelchy step towards him, 'if you want to know about the damned guest list why ask me? Ask Dad. I probably know half a dozen people here by first name. You're the one in the loop. I'm here to smile and take one for the team.'

'Take one for the team?'

'What else would you call it?' His outrage struck her as the height of hypocrisy. 'Apologies to your ego, but don't expect me to pretend I like the situation when we're alone!'

'No. You'll just pretend you haven't thought about what it will be like.'

'What *what* would be like?'

His slow predatory smile sent a pulse of sexual heat through her body.

'Oh, that.' She faked amusement to cover her embarrassment. 'Now? Here?' She laughed a high-pitched laugh. 'Has anyone ever mentioned your awful timing?'

'Actually, no.'

She swallowed hard, thinking, That I can believe. 'Silly me! Of course, even if you were lousy in bed they'd still tell you how marvellous you were because you're—' She broke off and finished lamely, 'You're...a prince.'

'You're a princess.'

'What?'

'You're a princess.'

As in dignified, serene, gracious, aloof...qualities that when she'd been plain old Hannah Latimer she'd had in abundance. Now she was the real deal—a real princess—she'd turned into some sort of fishwife!

It isn't me, it's him, she thought, levelling a look of breathless resentment up at his impossibly handsome face. He was the one who was making her act this way, the one who was making her feel...out of control. Because of him she was saying the first thing that popped into her head. She'd lost every vestige of mental censorship; she was saying things she didn't know she felt...

'Oh, God!' Without warning, the adrenalin wave that she'd been riding suddenly broke and she started shaking.

Watching her wrap her arms around herself, an action that didn't disguise the fact she was shaking like a leaf, Kamel felt a sharp stab of guilt. 'You've had a bad experience.' A fact he was a little late acknowledging.

She slung him a look. Anybody hearing him would think he gave a damn. 'I'm fine. Look, it was handy you turned up when you did.' He was the last person in the world she would have wanted to see her in that position, but that didn't alter the fact she had needed saving. 'And if the opportunity ever arises and some ex-girlfriend of yours comes to scratch your eyes out I'll return the favour.' By the time the last syllable had left her lips Hannah was utterly drained; her ironic smile was not weak, it was non-existent.

'So you will rescue me?' He was torn between amusement, astonishment and an uncharacteristic impulse that he firmly quashed. Comforting embraces were so *not* his style.

She felt the colour rush to her cheeks. 'You think that's funny because I'm a woman.' Hopping on one foot while she bent to try and retrieve the shoe that had been sucked into a patch of mud, she turned her head and threw him a look of frowning dislike. 'You going to stand there and watch?'

He held up his phone, his eyes trained on her bottom, the firm, curvy outline very clear against the silk of her gown. 'That really is a good look for you!'

'You dare!' she growled.

Still grinning—the grin made him look normal and nice and far too good-looking—he shrugged and slid the phone back into his pocket before he bent and grabbed the protruded strap of her shoe. It came free with a massive slurping sound.

'Well, Cinderella, you can go to the ball but I don't think that you're going to be doing much dancing in this,' he said, shaking free the larger dollops of mud that clung to the heel. His brows suddenly lifted.

'What?'

'I never realised,' he said, his glance transferring from the wrecked shoe to her foot and back again, 'that you actually have really big feet.'

Hannah's jaw dropped.

'As for women being weaker...Have you ever *seen* a tigress protecting her young?' It was not the image of a tigress that formed in his mind, though. It was Hannah with a baby in her arms at her breast.

'I suppose you have.' There was an air of resignation in her response. He'd done all the things she hadn't... An image that she had seen in a magazine during her last hairdresser's appointment superimposed itself over his face: the gorgeous scantily clad model strutting her stuff at a red-carpet event while her escort looked on indulgently.

'I have no doubt that a woman can be fierce in defence of what she considers hers.'

'You're not mine,' she blurted, embarrassed by the suggestion and slightly queasy. In her head the damned supermodel was now doing things to the man she had married that Hannah knew she never could...which was a good thing, she reminded herself.

'And I'm not fierce. I'm...I just like to pay my debts.'

'And you shall.'

Promise, threat...Hannah was beyond differentiating between the two even in her own head. 'By having sex with you?'

Anger drew the skin tight across his hard-boned features. 'I have no intention of negotiating sex with my own wife,' he asserted proudly.

'You think I'm going to have sex with a man I don't like or respect?' She barely spoke above a whisper but her low voice sounded loud in the charged silence.

'You don't have to respect or like someone to want to rip off their clothes.'

'My God, you do love yourself.'

'This isn't love, but it is a strong mutual attraction.'

Heart thudding, she dodged his stare and snatched the shoe from him, grimacing as she slid her foot back in. 'Thank you.' She managed two steps before the heel snapped and threw her off balance. The jolt as she struggled to stay upright caused her chignon to come free, effectively blinding her. She took several more lopsided strides forward before she stopped and swore.

Throwing him a look that dared him to comment, she took off both shoes and threw them in a bush. Hitching her skirt a little higher, she continued barefoot, feeling his eyes in her back.

'Go on, say it!' she challenged him.

'Say what?'

'Say whatever sarcastic little gem you're just

aching to say. Go ahead,' she said, opening her arms wide in invitation. 'I can take it.'

Their eyes connected and her challenging smile vanished. She dropped her arms so fast she almost lost her balance. She would have lowered her gaze had his dark, glittered stare not held her captive. The silence settled like a heavy velvet blanket around them. She had to fight for breath and fight the weird compulsion that made her want to…

'You want to take me, *ma belle*?' His eyes cancelled out the joke in his voice.

She could feel the heat inside her swell and she thought, Yes, I do. 'You can't say things like that to me.'

'What do you expect? You are a very confrontational woman.'

'I'm cold.'

'So the rumour goes, but we both know different. What were you doing with a man who wants to put you on a pedestal and worship you from afar?'

'Many girls dream of that.'

'Not you, though. You want to be touched and

you looked like you'd seen a ghost when you saw him.' Kamel had made it his business to find out who the man was who was responsible for her shaken look.

Hannah heaved in a deep breath. She *longed* to be touched. She shivered; he saw it and frowned. 'You're cold.'

'Oh, and I was just getting used to the idea of being hot,' she quipped back.

He threw her a look. 'I will explain to the guests that you are feeling unwell. Rafiq will see you to your room.'

On cue the big man appeared. Hannah was getting used to it—she didn't jump, but she did accept with gratitude the wrap he placed across her shoulders.

CHAPTER EIGHT

HANNAH ACTUALLY PERSUADED Rafiq to leave her in the hallway and made her way upstairs alone. It was an area of the house that no guests had entered and it was very quiet. She found herself walking past the door to the guest suite, drawn by a need to experience the comfort of familiar things. She took the extra flight of narrow winding oak stairs hidden behind a door that led up to the next floor.

The attic rooms had been the servants' quarters years before. Later on they became the nursery and more recently a semi self-contained unit, complete with mini kitchen. She opened the door of her old bedroom and stepped inside. The paintwork was bright and fresh but it was the same colour scheme she had chosen when she was twelve. The bed was piled high with stuffed toys, and the doll's house she had had for her tenth birthday stood on the table by the window. It was like being caught in a time warp.

She picked up a stuffed toy from the pile on the bed and flicked the latch on the doll's house. The door swung open, automatically illuminating the neat rooms inside.

She stood there, a frown pleating her brow, and waited. She didn't even recognise she was waiting until nothing happened. There was no warm glow, no lessening of tension. She didn't feel safe or secure.

In the past, she realised, this room had represented a sanctuary. She had closed the door and shut out the world. But even though the familiar things that had given her a sense of security were still the same—she had changed.

She closed the door of the doll's house with a decisive click. It was time to look forward, not back.

In the guest suite she showered and pulled a matching robe on over her silk pyjamas. Her hair hung loose and damp down her back. Leaving the steamy bathroom, she walked across to the interconnecting door and, after a pause, turned the key. Locked doors were no solution. Hugging a teddy bear had not helped, and hiding from the situation was not going to make it go away. Would talking help? Hannah didn't know, but she was willing to give it a try.

So long as he didn't construe the open door as an invitation to do more than talk.

She cinched the belt of her robe tight and walked across to the bed, trying not to think about the flare of sexual heat in her stomach as she heard his voice in her mind—*You don't have to respect or like someone to want to rip off their clothes.*

'Oh, God!'

She didn't know if the dismayed moan was in her head or she'd actually cried out, but when she opened her eyes there was no room for debate—he was no creation of her subconscious. A very real Kamel stood framed in the doorway, one shoulder wedged against the jamb, as he pulled his tie free from his neck.

'I'm glad that's over.'

He sounded almost human. He *was* human,

she realised, noticing the lines of fatigue etched into his face—a fatigue that was emphasised by the shadow of dark stubble across his jaw. So he could get tired. It was a tiny chink in his armour, but she still struggled to see him suffering the same doubts and fears as the rest of the human race, and it went without saying that fatigue didn't stop him looking stupendously attractive. No, *beautiful*, she corrected, her eyes running over the angles and planes of his darkly lean face, a face that she found endlessly fascinating. She compressed her lips and closed a door on the thought. She knew it would be foolish to lower her defences around him.

He pulled the tie through his long fingers and let it dangle there, arching a sardonic brow as his dark eyes swept her face. 'So, no locked doors?'

'That was childish.'

The admission surprised him but he hid it. It was harder to hide his reaction to the way she looked. The only trace of make-up was the pink varnish on her toenails. With her hair hanging damply down her back and her face bare she looked incredibly young, incredibly vulnerable and incredibly beautiful.

There was a wary caution in the blue eyes that met his, but not the hostility that he had come to expect.

'I thought you'd be asleep by now.' The purple smudges under her eyes no longer smoothed away by a skilful application of make-up made it clear she still desperately needed sleep. Kamel reminded himself that her nightmare had been going on forty-eight hours longer than his. He felt a flash of grudging admiration for her— whatever else the woman he had married was, she was not weak.

Hannah absently rubbed the toes of one foot against the arch of the other until she saw him staring and she tucked them under her. She pushed her hair behind her ears as she admitted, 'I felt bad letting you make excuses for me. Was it awkward?' She had probably broken about a hundred unwritten rules of protocol.

'Awkward?' He arched a brow. 'You mean did anyone see you leave with—?'

'I didn't leave with him. He f—'

He held up his hands in a gesture of surrender. 'I know.'

'Me not being there. What did you say?'

'I did not go into detail. I simply told my uncle that you had retired early.' He had actually told Charles Latimer a little more. He had made it clear to his father-in-law that if he wanted his daughter to spend any time under his roof he would guarantee that Rob Preston would not be there.

'Did they believe you?'

He took a step into the room and dropped his tie onto a chair. 'Why should we care?'

The *we* was not symbolic of some new togetherness so the small glow of pleasure it gave her was totally out of proportion.

'So how long were you standing there watching?' She had gone through the scene enough times to realise that Kamel could have heard some, if not all, of the exchange with Rob.

Grave-eyed, she looked up from her contemplation of her hands and heard him say, 'Long enough.'

She ground her teeth in exasperation at this deliberately cryptic response.

'So he cheated on you?'

Oh, yes, he would have heard that bit.

'It happens.'

There was no pity in his voice; Hannah let out a tiny sigh of relief.

'Dumping him on the actual wedding day was a pretty good revenge.' Kamel understood the attraction of retribution, though, being a man to whom patience did not come easily, he struggled with the concept of a dish served cold.

'I didn't plan it.' She looked startled by the idea. 'That's when I found out.'

He looked at her incredulously. 'On the actual day?'

She nodded, experiencing the familiar sick feeling in the pit of her stomach as the memory surfaced. It had been an hour before the photographers, hairdressers and make-up artists were due to arrive. She had knocked on Sal's door under the pretext of collecting the something blue her best friend had promised her, though what she had actually wanted was reassurance—

someone to tell her she was suffering from last-minute nerves and it was all normal.

'I walked in on him with Sal, my chief brides-maid. They were… It wasn't until later that I discovered he'd worked his way through most of my circle.'

She didn't look at him to see his reaction. She told herself she was past caring whether she came across as self-pitying and pathetic, but it wasn't true. She simply didn't have the strength left to maintain the illusion. The last few days one hit after another combined with exhaustion had destroyed her normal coping mechanisms… What pride she had left had been used up in her encounter with Rob.

'So he slept with everyone but you.'

Her eyes flew to his face. 'So you heard that too.'

He nodded. He had heard, but not quite under-stood. It was not a new strategy, and she was the sort of woman who was capable of inspiring ob-session in susceptible men, though why a man who was willing to marry to get a woman in his bed would then choose to sleep around was more difficult to understand. Especially when the woman in question would make all others look like pale imitations.

'So the only way he could have you was marriage.' Twenty-four hours ago the discovery would not have left him with a sense of disappointment. Twenty-four hours ago he'd had no expectations that could be disappointed—he had only expected the worst of her.

His cynical interpretation caused her cobalt-blue eyes to fly wide open in shocked horror. 'No, I wanted to.' She gave a tiny grimace and added more honestly, 'I would have.' The fact was she simply wasn't a very sexual creature, which did beg the question as to why she couldn't look at Kamel or even hear his voice without feeling her insides melt. 'But he...'

Kamel watched her fumble for words, looking a million miles from the controlled woman reputed to have a block of ice for a heart, and felt something tighten in his chest.

'Apparently he wanted to worship me, not—'

'Take you to bed,' Kamel supplied, thinking the man was even more of a loser than he'd thought.

'I don't actually think he thought of me as a woman. More an addition to his art collection. He likes beautiful things...not that I'm saying I'm—'

'Don't spoil all this honesty by going coy. We both know you're beautiful. So why is it everyone thinks he's the injured party?'

'I'd prefer to be thought a bitch than an idiot.' The explanation was not one she had previously articulated. She was startled to hear the words. It was something she had not admitted to anyone before.

'And your father still invited the man here?' If a man had treated his daughter that way he would have— Kamel dragged a chair out from the dressing table, swung it around and straddled it.

'Oh, it was easier to let him think I'd had second thoughts. They've been friends for a long time and Dad had already had an awful time telling everyone the wedding was cancelled.

A lot of people turned up and it was terrible for him—'

'And you were having such a great day…'

Hannah's protective instincts surfaced at the implied criticism of her father.

'You were right. It was my fault. This is my fault, totally my fault.'

He shook his head, bemused by her vehemence, and protested, 'You didn't ask the guy to jump you!'

'No, not Rob. Getting arrested, getting you mixed up in it, terrifying Dad half to death. If he has another heart attack, it would be down to me.'

It was news to Kamel that he had had one. The man certainly hadn't been scared enough to change his lifestyle. 'I think a doctor might disagree. Your father does not hold back when it comes to saturated fat.'

'You're trying to make me feel better.'

He studied her face. 'It's clearly not working.'

'Why are you being nice? It's my fault we had to get married. I should have waited for help. I shouldn't have left the Land Rover. I shouldn't have been there at all.' She shook her head, her face settling into a mask of bitter self-recrimination as she loosed a fractured sob. 'All the things you said.'

'The village did get the vaccines, and the help they needed.'

Lost in a morass of self-loathing, she didn't seem to hear him. 'I couldn't even help myself, let alone anyone else. I was only there to prove a point. I've spent my life playing it safe.' She planted her hand flat on her heaving chest and lifted her tear-filled eyes to his.

'I always played by the rules. I even wanted a safe man… I didn't even have the guts to do what I really wanted.' She shook her head slowly from side to side and sniffed. 'I went to university and did a course I had absolutely no interest in rather than stand up to my dad. I got engaged to a man who seemed safe and solid, and when he turned out to be a total bastard did I learn? No, I got engaged to a man I knew would never hurt me because…I always go for the safe option.'

He let out a long, low whistle. '*Dieu*, I wanted

you to take responsibility for your own actions—not the financial crisis, world hunger and bad days in the week that have a Y in them.'

Startled, Hannah lifted her head. Her eyes connected with his and a small laugh was shaken from her chest. 'I just want...' She stopped, her husky voice suspended by tears, her control still unravelling so fast she could not keep pace.

With a muttered imprecation he dropped down to his knees beside the bed and pushed the hair back from her damp face.

'What do you want?'

Her wide brimming blue eyes lifted. 'I just want to be...to feel...not like this.' She gnawed at her lower lip and brought her lashes down in a protective veil. 'Sorry, I don't know why I'm saying this stuff to you.'

Responding to the painful tug in his chest, Kamel stood up and gently pushed her down. Sliding his hand behind her knees, he swung her legs onto the bed, pulling a pillow under her head before joining her.

'Go to sleep,' he said, lowering his long length onto the bed beside her.

'I can't sleep. I have dreams that I'm back in that cell and he is...' She struggled to sit up. A light touch on her breastbone stopped her rising and after a moment she stopped fighting. 'I can't sleep.'

He touched a finger to her lips. 'Move over.' Pausing to slide an arm under her shoulders, he pulled her head back onto his shoulder.

'Why are you being nice to me?' she whispered into his neck—and then a moment later she was asleep.

Kamel, who preferred his own bed, realised this was the first time in his life that he had slept with a woman, in the literal sense. Only he wasn't sleeping and he seriously doubted he would. A state of semi-arousal combined with seething frustration was not in his experience conducive to sleep, especially when there was zero chance of doing anything to relieve that frustration.

On the plus side at least the scenery was rather special. Asleep she looked like a wanton angel. There were probably a lot of men out there who would be willing to give up a night's sleep to look at that face. He was aware of an ache of desire somewhere deep inside him so strong it hurt. Ignoring it didn't make it go away, and not looking at her was not an option because his eyes, like the north arrow on a compass, kept going back to the same place.

So in the end he didn't question it; he just accepted it.

Hannah fought her way out of a dream, struggling to shake off the lingering sense of dread.

'Wake up. You're safe.'

Still half asleep, she opened her eyes, saw his face and sighed. 'I love your mouth,' she said before pressing her own lips to the sensual curve.

'Hannah.' He pulled away.

She blinked, the confusion slowly filtering from her.

'Sorry, I thought you were a dream.' She had kissed him and he hadn't kissed her back. He hadn't done anything. Once was bad, but twice was humiliating.

'I thought you were a bitch.' And that had made

the politically expedient marriage not right, but not this wrong. 'I was wrong.'

'Not a bitch.' Great, I feel so much better.

Suddenly she felt very angry. She struggled to sit up. 'So what is wrong with me?' she asked, looking down at him for once. 'I mean, there has to be, doesn't there? I've been engaged twice, and no sex.' Hannah could hear the words coming out of her mouth. She knew she shouldn't be saying them but she couldn't stop. 'Now I'm married, and you don't even want to kiss me!'

With a dry sob she flung herself down and rolled over, her back to him.

It was the sight of her heaving shoulders that snapped the last threads of Kamel's self-imposed restraint. 'Don't cry,' he begged.

'I'm not crying,' she retorted, sniffing. 'I've just realised something. I don't know why I was so bothered about marrying you.'

'I'm flattered.'

Hannah rolled over until she was able to stare straight at him. She had barely registered his dry comment, as her thoughts—dark ones—were turned inward.

'I can't even do sex so what would the point have been of waiting for someone who can give me...*more*?'

Kamel had never felt any driving desire to be a with a woman who considered him her soul mate. On the other hand, being basically told that you were an *all right* consolation prize for someone with low expectations was a bit below the belt even for someone with his ego.

Well at least the pressure is off, he thought. She's not expecting much of you!

His sudden laugh made her look up.

'So you are willing to settle for me?'

A small puzzled indent appeared between her feathery brows as she struggled to read his expression. 'Doesn't seem like I have a lot of choice in the matter, does it?' She glanced at the ring on her finger.

'So you are willing to...how did you put it— take one for the team?'

'I thought you'd have been glad to know that you don't have to pretend, that I don't expect—'

'Much?'

This drew an exasperated hiss from Hannah.

'Well, the mystery of why you're a virgin is solved,' he drawled. 'You talked them to sleep.'

With an angry snort Hannah reached behind her for one of the pillows that had been spread across the bed while she slept.

'I don't think so, angel.'

Somewhere between picking it up and lobbing it at him she found the pillow was removed from her fingers and a moment later she was lying with her wrists held either side of her head, with his body suspended above her.

She could hear a sound above the thunderous clamour of her frantic heartbeat—it was her panting. She couldn't draw enough air into her lungs to stop her head spinning. His mouth was a whisper away from hers; she could feel the warmth of his breath on her lips.

The dark intent shining in his heavy-lidded eyes made the heat prickle under her skin.

'Just—' he ran his tongue lightly across the surface of her lips '—how—' he kissed one corner of her mouth '—much—' he kissed the other corner, smiling as she gave a deep languid sigh and lifted her head towards him '—are you willing—' he kissed her full on her trembling lips before trailing a series of burning kisses down the smooth column of her neck '—to take for the team?'

'I...don't...God...stop...please don't stop!' she moaned, terrified at the thought he might.

Her beating heart stumbled as his beautiful mouth came crashing down to claim her lips. The relief she felt as she opened her mouth to him in silent invitation was quickly consumed by the response of her body to the thrust of his tongue: low in her belly each carnal incursion caused a tight clenching; between her legs the dampness ran hot.

While he kissed her with something approaching desperation his hands were busy in her hair, on her face, sliding under her nightdress to caress the warm skin of her smooth thighs then reaching to curve over one taut, tingling breast. As he found the loop of the top button and slipped it off his patience snapped and he tugged hard, causing the remainder to tear from the fabric as he pushed the two sides apart to reveal her breasts to his hungry stare.

She arched up into him as he took first one turgid rosy peak and then the other into his mouth, leaving her gasping and moaning; her entire body reached fever pitch in seconds. He pressed a kiss to her belly and the frustration building inside got higher and higher as his finger slid lower and lower, inscribing a tingling line between her aching breasts and then down her quivering belly.

Nakedness turned out not to be inhibiting—it was liberating. She lifted her arms and tugged him down to her. The slow, drugging kisses continued as she arched, pushing her breasts up against his hard chest, frantic for skin-to-skin contact. Her hands ran down the strong, smooth lines of his back, revealing his strength, his sleek hardness.

The liquid heat in her belly had a new urgency as he began to fumble with the buckle on his belt. A moment later she heard the sound of his zipper.

Afflicted by a belated bout of virginal modesty, she closed her eyes, opening them only when he took her hands in his and curled them around the hot, silky, rock-hard erection.

She couldn't prevent the little gasp that was wrenched from somewhere in her chest.

At least make an effort to look like you know what you're doing, Hannah.

The voice in her head was critical but he was not.

A deep feral moan was wrenched from his throat as her fingers began to experimentally tighten then release the pressure around the throbbing column. His eyes drifted shut and he began to breathe hard. Then without warning he took her hand and tipped her back onto the pillows.

She let out a series of fractured gasps that terminated in a higher-pitched wailing moan as he touched the dampness between her thighs.

'This is good?' he slurred thickly as he continued to stroke and torment, making her ache everywhere.

She nodded vigorously and pushed against the heel of his hand. 'Oh, yes…very good.'

He raised himself up, took her hand and, holding her gaze, laid it against his chest. Not looking away from her eyes for an instant, he fought his way out of his shirt and flung it away.

'You're beautiful,' she breathed, unable to take her greedy stare off his tautly muscled, gleaming torso.

Kamel swallowed. He wanted her badly. At that moment he could not think of anything he had wanted more.

'I've wanted to be inside you since the moment I saw you.' He pushed against her, letting her share the relentless ache in his groin.

'I want that too.' Delighting in the discovery of an inherent sensuality, she parted her thighs.

Responding to the silent invitation with a fierce groan, he came over her and settled between her legs. She had expected to tense at that final point of no return, but she relaxed. It was easy, not so painful as she'd imagined—and then as her body tightened around him she felt her blood tingle and squeezed her eyelids tight, just focusing on all the things that were happening inside and Kamel filling her so wonderfully, Kamel moving, pushing her somewhere...

Then just as the itch got too intense to bear, she found out where she was going and let go. She heard Kamel cry out, felt the flood of his release and wrapped her legs around him, afraid that she'd be washed away, lost.

She wasn't. She finished up where she'd started, under Kamel.

Some time later she did recover the power of speech but she couldn't do full sentences.

'Wow!' she said, staring at the ceiling. Beside her, his chest heaving, Kamel was doing the same.

He turned his head. 'For a first effort, I have to say you show promise.'

This time he did not prevent her lobbing the pillow at his head, but in the subsequent tussle it ended on the floor and they ended up in a tangle of limbs.

CHAPTER NINE

WHEN HANNAH WOKE it was light and she was alone.

She felt the bed beside her—it was still warm. She gave a wistful sigh. She hadn't expected him to be there but it would have been…no, *nice* was not part of their relationship. Though yesterday she would have said the same about sex. It was crazy, in a good way, that the area of this marriage she'd thought would be hardest—that she had been dreading—turned out to be the easiest and the most pleasurable.

She gave a voluptuous sigh and smiled. It had been easy, natural, and totally incredible.

She sat up suddenly, her eyes flying wide in dawning alarm. She was assuming that it would be happening again soon and often. But what if last night wasn't going to be something that happened regularly? While she hadn't known what she was missing, celibacy had been easy—but now she did know. She gave an anxious sigh.

It would be…terrible. One night and Kamel was her drug of choice; she was a total addict.

She showered and dressed in record time, wondering if she should just come out and ask him. She was on her way to see Sarah when she literally bumped into him. He was dressed in running shorts and a tee shirt and looked so gorgeous that she was struck dumb.

'I've been running.'

She nodded, and thought that there really was such a thing as being paralysed with lust. If she'd stayed in bed, would he have walked in? Her eyelids drooped as she imagined him peeling off his top and—

'And you are…?' he prompted.

Hannah started guiltily, the colour rushing to her cheeks. 'I'm going to see Sarah, and Olive and the puppies.'

'Sarah?'

'The cook…but she's more than that. I'll be ready for the flight.'

'I'm sure you will. See you then.'

He actually saw her much sooner. He had showered and was beginning to wade through his emails when he heard her bedroom door slam, quite loudly. A slamming door was not in itself indicative of a problem. He cut off the pointless line of speculation and focused on work. Luckily his ability to ignore distractions was almost as legendary as his reputation for zero patience for those undisciplined individuals who brought their personal lives into the workplace.

Five minutes later he closed his laptop, realising that in the interests of efficiency it would save time if he just went and checked she was all right.

He didn't ask. It was obvious she wasn't.

'What's wrong?'

Hannah stopped pacing and turned around. 'Nothing.'

He arched a brow.

'I can't tell you.' She pressed a fist to her mouth.

He walked over, removed her fist and said calmly, 'What can't you tell me?'

'I walked in on Sarah with Dad, They were...' her eyes slid towards the bed '...you know.'

Kamel blinked. 'You walked in on your father having sex with the cook?'

She covered her ears with her hands. 'Don't say it out loud!'

Kamel fought back a smile. 'It always comes as a shock to a child when they learn their parents have sex.'

'I know my father has sex. I just don't want to see it!'

This time he couldn't fight the smile. 'It's going to be tough for him—'

'No, they didn't see me. That really would be awful. No, the door was half open and...' She stopped, closed her eyes and shook her head, shuddered. 'I backed out and ran.'

'I imagine you did.' His lips quivered.

'This isn't funny,' she protested.

Unable to stop himself, Kamel began to laugh.

A laugh bubbled in her throat. 'I want to delete the image from my mind. I really do.' The laugh escaped.

Five minutes later Hannah was all laughed out,

and Kamel was sprawled on the bed, one arm under his head, telling her that when he had walked in he had thought there had been some major disaster.

'Your face! Honestly it was...' He sat up and sighed. 'I should get back to it. I've got a stack of—'

'I'm sorry I stopped you working.'

He gave a sudden grin. 'No, you're not.' He patted the bed beside him and leaned back against the pillows.

Hannah came across the room, hesitating only a moment before she manoeuvred herself to sit straddling him.

'I like your thinking,' he purred, his eyes flaring hot as she pulled the top over her head. 'I like other things even more.'

'Are you all right?'

Hannah shrugged and put down the book she had been holding. Her interest in the novel was feigned but her confusion was not. 'With flying, you mean...?'

A spasm of irritation crossed his face. 'Your

father and the cook? It happens—the attraction between people from different backgrounds.'

Her brow smoothed and she laughed. 'You think I didn't know? Or that I have some sort of problem with it?'

His brows lifted. 'You are telling me you don't?'

In defiance of his open scepticism, she shook her head from side to side. 'Beyond the fact that discovering that your parent has a sex life, which is a bit…uncomfortable…no, I like Sarah.'

'And the fact she is the cook?'

'I know you think I'm a snob. She's probably the best thing that has ever happened to my dad. I just wish he… I wish they'd come out into the open about it. I wish…' She caught the expression on Kamel's face and, taking it for boredom, brought her ramble to a juddering stop.

It would be a massive mistake to assume that, because Kamel had seemed to have an endless fascination with her body, his interest extended beyond the bedroom. She knew that any woman would only ever be a substitute for the woman he had lost, Amira. Kamel must have thought nothing could be worse than seeing the woman he loved happy with another man—until he'd found out that there was something much worse.

'You wish?'

I wish I could look at you and not ache. 'Forget it.'

It was sex—fantastic, incredible sex—but she had to stop thinking about it.

'I don't want to bore you.'

He unclipped his seat belt and stretched his long legs out in front of him. 'Don't worry. If you bore me I'll let you know,' he promised.

'I think that Sarah deserves more than to be a secret…' She gave a self-conscious shrug.

'Maybe this Sarah is happy with just sex.'

She looked away. Was there a message, a warning even, in there for her?

'Maybe she is,' Hannah agreed without conviction. She turned her head to angle a curious look at his face. 'You expected me to be devastated to find my father in bed with the cook, didn't you? Sarah has been my father's mistress for the past five years that I know of. Probably longer.

'The truth is I've no idea how Sarah is content to be treated like some sort of...' She stopped, wondering whether that wasn't exactly what she was doing. 'We both worry about her.'

'We?'

'Sarah's daughter, Eve, and I. She's a year younger than me.' She noticed the airstrip below and pressed her face to the window to get a better view. 'Is it far to the villa?'

'Not by helicopter.'

'Helicopter?'

He nodded. 'It beats being stuck in a traffic jam.'

That, she thought, was a matter of opinion.

As the helicopter landed Hannah closed her eyes—but even with them squeezed tightly shut she retained the stomach-clenching image of them falling directly into the ocean.

The pilot landed the helicopter smoothly but Hannah appeared oblivious, her eyes tightly shut, hands clenched into white-knuckled fists. Her lips continued to move, presumably in a silent prayer. Watching her silent but abject terror, he had felt like an inconsiderate monster for subjecting her to what had clearly been an ordeal. He wanted to be irritated with her but she looked so fragile, her big eyes reminding him of a scared child. But she wasn't a child. She was all woman—*his* woman. The reminder should have made him feel resentful—after all, he was paying the price for her stupidity—but instead the thought came with an accompanying shaft of possessive pride.

'You can breathe now.'

Hannah opened her eyes and collided instantly with Kamel's dark, intense stare. The feeling of falling into the abyss didn't go away; if anything it intensified as, with a thudding heart, she fumbled with her seat belt.

'What time is it?' she heard herself ask.

'You have somewhere you need to be, *ma belle*?' His eyes drifted to the wide, full, plump curve of her lips and he felt the barely damped fires of passion roar into life.

She was the most responsive woman he had ever had in his bed. He still couldn't get his head around the fact that the cool, distant virgin had turned out to be a warm, giving woman who held nothing back. In the middle of figuring how long he could wait until he got her into bed again he found himself wondering about the sequence of events that had led her to hide her passionate nature behind a cool mask.

He had never felt the need to look beyond the surface of a beautiful woman, and he had no intention of looking too far now.

'Relax.'

This struck Hannah as ironic advice from someone who, as far as she could tell, never totally switched off, someone who was never *totally* off duty. Duty always came first with Kamel. If it didn't, they wouldn't be married.

While Kamel was speaking to the pilot she took the opportunity to look through the glass without fear of gibbering. The helipad was not, as it had seemed, positioned perilously on the cliff's edge, but several hundred feet away, and screened from the villa by an avenue of trees. Hannah could just make out through the branches the terracotta roof, but the rest of the villa was totally concealed by the lush greenery.

Above the whirr of the blades she could hear the men's voices. She was struggling to catch what they were saying when it happened. Previously it had only occurred when she was in a small space—the lift between floors, or in the pantry in the kitchen—but now there were no walls to close in on her, just glass. Even so, the urge to escape and the struggle to breathe were equally strong.

Her knees were shaking but Hannah was so anxious to get back on terra firma that she didn't wait. She didn't wait for Kamel, who was still deep in conversation with the pilot; she just had to get out of there.

Hannah watched as her luggage was piled onto a golf cart by two men—one of whom she had almost flattened when she missed the bottom step in her anxiety to escape the helicopter. Both men nodded respectfully to Kamel and vanished through an arch cut in the neatly trimmed green foliage.

Hannah could feel Kamel's disapproval—she'd sensed it before but it had upped several notches.

'You should have said that you have a problem with helicopters.' Seeing the surprise in the blue eyes that flew to his face, he smiled. 'Yes, it was obvious.' He took one of her hands in his and turned the palm upwards, exposing the grooves her nails had cut into her palms. 'Any tenser and I think you'd have snapped. Why on earth didn't you say anything?'

'Why didn't you ask?' she countered, wishing he would release her hand, while feeling an equally strong reluctance to break the contact. His thumb was moving in circles across her palm, and each light, impersonal caress sent wave after wave of disproportionate pleasure through her body. But then there was no sense of proportion in her response to Kamel when she thought about how completely and how quickly she had given up control, and it terrified her.

She tensed as his eyes flicked from her palm to her face. 'You have a point,' he conceded. 'Should I call them back?' He gestured in the direction of the now invisible carts. 'I thought you might like to stretch your legs, but if you prefer—?'

'No, a walk would be good.' A night of mind-

blowing sex might be better, though. The recip-
rocal warm glow in his eyes made her wonder
if underneath all the politeness an alternative
dialogue wasn't just going on in his own head
too. But who knew what went on in the mind of
a man like Kamel?

She couldn't begin to intellectualise her response to him. How could she be standing here,
thinking about him ripping her clothes off?

Shocked and more than a little excited by the
thought, she lowered her gaze. 'You don't have
to act as though this is a real honeymoon,' she
murmured. It was duty for him. And for her it
was…all so new she had no name for what she
was feeling. But the ferocity of it scared her. 'I
know it's window dressing.' It had never crossed
her mind that she could want a man's touch this
badly, to the extent it was hard to think past it.

'I like touching you.'

For a shocked instant she thought she had
voiced her secret longing. 'Oh!'

'The sex wasn't window dressing.'

Experiencing a wave of lust so immense she
felt as though she were drowning, she closed her

fingers tight around his hand. She swallowed, suddenly unable to meet his eyes, her heart thudding fast in her chest. She felt bizarrely shy. The emotion paralysed her vocal cords and brought a rosy flush to her cheeks.

'We are expected to make a baby, so why not enjoy it?'

The glow faded. Afterwards, with his duty done, would he seek his pleasure elsewhere? His life was all duty—he would probably be glad to escape it.

'It's not far to the villa,' he said as they reached the top of the incline they had been climbing.

Hannah gasped. 'It's beautiful, Kamel.'

'Yes,' he agreed. 'So, you think you might be able to stick it here for a few days?'

How few? she wondered. And what happened after that? But then she closed down that line of thought. Better to enjoy the here and now and not think too far ahead.

'I might cope.' She looked at the sugar-pink painted villa that seemed to cling to the edge of the cliff.

'I even know where the kitchen is here.'

She lifted her brows and tried to look serious but a laugh bubbled through. 'I'm more interested in the pool today.' She mimed a fanning gesture with her hand.

'That sounds good.' He withdrew the vibrating phone from his pocket and looked at the screen. 'Sorry, I might have to take a rain check on that.' You did not hang up on a king, even—or maybe especially—if that king was your uncle. 'I really have to take this. Go have an explore.'

Hannah nodded, lowering her eyes to hide the irrational stab of hurt. It was crazy to mind that she was not at the top of his priorities.

CHAPTER TEN

WHEN SHE SLID open the wardrobes that lined one wall of the dressing room and found they weren't empty, Hannah thought she was seeing an example of Kamel's famed forward thinking.

The beginnings of a frown began to form on her brow as she lifted the top item on the stack of underclothes. Size-wise—not to mention style-wise—it was really not her! A few moments later as she flicked through the row of expensive garments the frown was fully formed and it had become obvious that even Kamel did not think of everything! She felt her self-righteous anger reach new heights as she picked up the faint but distinctive scent that clung to the garments. He thought it was fine to have his wife share wardrobe space with his mistress…maybe the economy appealed to him!

She felt physically sick, but, in the grip of a

masochistic urge she could not fight, Hannah stretched out a shaking hand to the neatly folded stacks of underclothes on the shelf. They were not items that could be classed utilitarian or, by any stretch of the imagination, tasteful.

Hannah pushed the lot onto the floor and, with a vengeful cry, grabbed the most tacky, glittering thing she could see. It turned out to be a gold beaded dress with a designer label, and a split so low on the back the wearer couldn't possibly have worn any underclothes.

Had she been this angry when she discovered Rob's multiple infidelities? Hannah was incapable by this point of questioning the degree of her reaction. She was incandescent with rage. Not only did she not want a second-hand G-string, she didn't want a second-hand man!

How stupid had she been to even begin to let down her guard with him, to trust him? Experience had taught her you couldn't trust a man.

Eyes flashing, back stiff, she stalked down the glass-roofed corridor that connected the more modern bedroom wing to the main house and into the open-plan living room where she had left Kamel. The room was empty but the echoing sound of her heels on the terracotta tiles drew a call from outside.

'Come have a swim!'

Responding to the invitation with narrow-eyed determination, she exited the patio doors just as Kamel levered himself from the infinity pool.

Rising in one seamless motion, he stood with the towel he had retrieved from the pool's edge in one hand, but he made no attempt to dry himself. The water continued to stream down his lean brown body, making his skin glisten like polished copper in the sun.

She caught her breath. Not even a full-blown rage could protect her from her visceral reaction to the sight of six feet four inches of dripping-wet Kamel. She was helpless to control her quivering response to the image of earthy power in his broad shoulders, deeply muscled chest, and strong thighs. She swallowed, knowing she was staring but helpless to stop herself. The moisture clinging to his skin emphasised each individual slab of muscle in his flat washboard torso, and he didn't carry an ounce of surplus flesh to blur the perfect muscle definition.

Kamel was all hard, primal male; he represented a physical male ideal combined with an earthy sexuality that had made him a deadly combination—the perfect lover. As she stared at him Hannah could feel her anger slipping away, feel the heat build inside her. She sucked in a short shocked breath, her eyes widening in disgust with herself as she recognised what was happening.

He looped the towel around his neck and she turned her head slightly to avoid the rippling contraction that moved across his flat torso as he lifted his arm to drag a hand across his wet hair.

She would *not* turn into one of those women who put up with all sorts of crap from a man just because he was…well…good in bed. And Kamel was, in her defence. There were probably not enough superlatives to describe just *how* good he was! She smothered the internal sigh and thought that he'd certainly had enough practice at it. It was not by accident they had dubbed him The *Heartbreaker* Prince!

One corner of his sensual mouth lifted in a lazy half-smile, but there was nothing lazy about the gleam in his eyes. She pressed a hand to her stomach—not that it helped to calm the fluttering.

'I think you're a little overdressed, angel,' he rasped throatily.

The same could not be said of him. The black shorts he wore low on his hips left little to the imagination—and hers was rioting as she raised the level of her stare.

'There are some swimsuits in the pool house.'

She closed her mouth with a firm and audible snap. Clutching the dress in one hand and her anger in the other, she slung him a contemptuous look that would have frozen a normal man stone dead in his tracks. The man she had married gave a here-we-go-again look and dragged some of the excess moisture from his hair with one hand, sending a shower of silver water droplets over her heated skin.

'I just bet there are, but I'm not too keen on wearing other women's cast-offs—or, for that matter, sleeping with them!'

He responded to her hostility with a long, slow, considering look. *'Right.'*

He didn't add *I see* because he didn't. When she had left him a few minutes earlier the sexual promise in her blue eyes… Well, if she hadn't left when she had, he had been within an undiplomatic hair's breadth of doing the unthinkable—slamming the phone down on his uncle with the explanation, *I need to make love to my wife.*

Acknowledging the strength of that need had been what had driven him to the pool. He hadn't spared his body—the relentless pace through the water should have left him incapable of breath, let alone lust, but the ache was still there, and now she was looking at him as though he had just been found guilty of waging a hate campaign against kittens!

He ground his teeth at the sheer, unremitting frustration of it all. He tilted his head, a dark scowl forming on his wide forehead as he fished for a word that summed up his life before Hannah had come into it. *Centred.*

At another time he might have appreciated the

black irony of the situation, but at that moment, with frustrated desire clenched like a knot, the humour passed him by. He had married her, resenting both the sense of duty that made him step up and the woman herself. And now, days later, he wanted her so badly he could barely string a coherent thought together. He was utterly consumed by it.

Not his type…well, that self-delusion had lasted about five seconds! Hannah was every man's type and once you saw the woman behind the cool mask… He shook his head, his fine-tuned steel trap of a mind finding it impossible to rationalise the fascination she exerted for him, the all-consuming need he felt to possess her and to lose himself in her.

It was just sex, he told himself, recognising an uncharacteristic tendency to over-analyse in his train of thought. Why try and read anything else into it? He'd married a woman he couldn't keep his hands off. But there was always a flip side, no heaven without hell. Not only did she have the ability to stretch the boundaries of sexual pleasure, she also had the ability to drive him crazy with her mood swings.

He forced his eyes from her face to the garment in her hand. Her mood seemed out of proportion with a wardrobe malfunction. He struggled to school his features into something that conveyed an interest he did not feel—he was more interested in peeling off her clothes than discussing fashion.

'You want to show me a new dress?'

Her brows hit her hairline. He actually thought she wanted to parade around and ask his approval!

'I suppose you've never seen this before?' Her voice shook almost as much as her hand did as she held out the backless, frontless, totally tasteless garment.

Recognition clicked in his brain. 'I have.' He had little interest in women's clothes but this one had been hard to forget—as was the evening that had gone with it.

He hadn't been the intended victim or beneficiary of the provocative number. Neither, it turned out, had Charlotte begged him to escort her to the glittering premiere for the pleasure of his company. He and the dress had been part of her revenge on her ex-husband. Bizarrely, although Charlotte had been glad to be out of her marriage, she had resented the fact her ex had moved on too—especially as the woman he had moved on to was a younger version of herself.

'You're angry.' His eyes slid down her body, over the slim curves and long, long legs. She was, he decided, totally magnificent. 'I know because your eyes turn from summer sky to stormy sea when you're mad.'

'It can work once, even twice, but I have to tell you, Kamel, that the staring-deep-into-my-eyes thing has a shelf life,' she lied. 'So don't try and change the subject.'

'What was the subject?' he asked, continuing to stare deep into her eyes, causing major and probably permanent damage to her frazzled nervous system.

'Your girlfriend's choice of clothes. Oh, incidentally, I'm *totally* fine with sharing my wardrobe space with your harem, though I have to tell you that they are not my size!'

'I know,' he said, his fingertips twitching as he transferred his stare to Hannah's heaving breasts. They fitted almost perfectly into his palms, soft, firm and... He took a deep swallow and lifted his gaze. 'Charlotte has had help in that area. They were, I believe, an engagement present from her ex.'

Her chin went up as she enquired in a deceptively soft voice, 'Are you suggesting I need help in that area?'

The icy question drew a low smoky laugh from him. 'You are *perfect* in that area.' The humour faded from his face, leaving a restless hunger. She was perfect. His perfect lover.

The hunger in his stare as much as his flattering words brought hot colour flying to her cheeks. But this heat was mild compared to the surge of sexual warmth that settled deep in her pelvis and spread. Her mask of disdain was rice-paper thin as she gave a sniff and tossed her head.

'I have no interest,' she informed him icily. 'Not in what your idea of perfect is, or the surgical procedures your girlfriend has had, or who paid for them.' Her haughty delivery vanished as the strength of her feelings became impossible to disguise. 'I just have an interest in being treated with a modicum, a bare *modicum* of respect while we are sharing a—' on the brink of saying bed, she stopped herself; the chain of thought already set in motion was less easy to stall '—roof!' she improvised, seeing his muscled body sleek with sweat, his face taut in a mask of need.

'I'm sorry you were upset. I gave instructions for the room to be cleared.'

'Cleared!' she parroted, her face twisted in an ironic grimace of disgust. 'I would have thought *fumigated* would have been more appropriate when we're talking about the sort of woman who would wear this!' She directed a look of lip-curling distaste at the garment, which was a perfect example of the adage money couldn't buy class.

'Don't you think you're overreacting to what is, after all, a simple housekeeping error? I'll speak to someone and it won't happen again.'

'You mean the next time your girlfriend leaves her clothes you'll have them tidied away *before*

I arrive? My God,' she flung with sarcastic appreciation. 'I'm one hell of a lucky woman to have married such a considerate man.'

'I will not be seeing Charlotte again.' Though the lady had made it quite clear that she did not see marriage as an obstacle to continuing their relationship.

'I do not want to know her name.' Or hear how good she is in bed, Hannah thought, experiencing a wave of jealousy that felt like a knife between her ribs. She paled and lifted her hands to her ears, squeezing her eyes shut.

Unfortunately neither action blotted out the knowledge that there would be women in slutty outfits sharing his bed in the future. They just wouldn't be called Charlotte.

She drew in a deep shuddering breath, her temper reaching boiling point in the time it took her to drag air into her lungs. 'So you think I'm *overreacting*?' she quivered incredulously. 'I'm curious—are you *trying* to be an insensitive, hateful slob?'

I'm curious—are you trying to look like a tart?
Kamel laughed as he recalled his response to

Charlotte in the dress his bride held in a death grip. But then he saw Hannah's face. 'I'm not laughing at you.'

'Oh, you're laughing with me. I feel *so* much better.'

His jaw clenched as he fought to contain his increasing irritation. Sexual frustration had already eaten deep chunks out of his self-control without his dealing with her emotional antics. He took a deep breath and decided he would rise above it and be reasonable, even if she wasn't!

'I wasn't thinking about you. I was thinking about Charlotte.'

If Kamel ever found himself faced with an angry and unreasonable woman he generally removed himself from that scene. By choice he avoided women likely to indulge in scenes, but you couldn't always tell and it paid to have a plan B.

He should have walked. She was asking him to explain his actions, and no woman had ever done that.

Looking into her eyes was like staring straight into a storm. Though storms were preferable to thinking too much about the flash of desperate hurt he had seen in those shimmering depths. Crazily, of all the emotions he was struggling to contain the one that rose to the surface— the compelling urge to wipe that hurt away. It made no sense. It had been her decision to enact a Greek tragedy when given the same circumstances most women would have chosen to tactfully ignore it.

'Look. I'm sorry that the room was not cleared. I'll have t—'

'You're crazy if you think I am going to sleep in that bedroom with you!'

His jaw tightened. 'You know something? I'm starting to feel quite nostalgic for Hannah the ice queen.' He jammed his thumbs into the waistband of his shorts and glared at her. 'Just what is your problem, anyway? I had a sex life before we were married.' He lifted one shoulder in a half-shrug. 'Having sex does not make me some sort of weird pervert. Most people would think that it makes me a lot more normal than a woman who is so uptight and controlling that she saves herself for marriage.'

'So now I'm not normal? Well, let me ease your mind on one thing. I sure as hell wasn't waiting for you!'

'And yet, you can't get enough of me in bed.'

'It's the novelty value.'

He clenched his teeth and glared at the gold gown in her hands. 'Give me that damned thing.'

She looked into his dark eyes and felt the answering passions surface. Heart thudding like a trip hammer, she ignored the hand extended to her and shook her head.

'You're being very childish. I have had other women. This can hardly be a surprise to you.'

Of course it wasn't—so why the hell was she acting like this?

'I don't give a damn about your girlfriends!' she contended, snapping her fingers to show how little she cared. 'You can have a damned harem for all I care!'

'I'm glad you explained that. So *this*—' his hand sketched a toe-to-head line in the air '—is someone who doesn't care a jot? If you hadn't explained I might,' he drawled, 'have thought it was jealousy.'

Her reaction to the suggestion was dramatic. The colour that had flooded her face receded, leaving her eyes a deep well of colour.

'This isn't jealousy,' she denied, trying desperately to think of an alternative and failing. 'This is wanting to be treated with respect.'

'Am I asking you to hide in the damned shadows?' The woman, he decided, took irrationality to new uncharted levels. 'This has gone on long enough. Hand it over.'

He caught the hem of the dress and Hannah responded with teeth-gritting determination, pulling it into her chest with such force she heard the sound of fabric tearing. She was clinging on so hard that when he pulled the dress she came with it.

To absorb the impact of her soft body into his, Kamel took an automatic step back and felt his foot hit the edge of the pool just as Hannah lifted her gaze.

She saw the intent gleaming in his dark eyes and shook her head. 'You wouldn't!'

His smile was answer enough.

She hit the water yelling a warning and spluttered as the water filled her nose and throat. His arm was wrapped around her waist as they both surfaced. When the water cleared from her eyes she saw he was laughing. She opened her mouth and Kamel pressed a hard kiss to it before he let go, kicking away from her.

She lifted a hand to her mouth. Thinking only of the kiss and not the fact there were several feet of water beneath her feet, she stopped treading water to stay afloat.

He waited for her to surface, breathless and angry and still, amazingly, clutching the damned dress.

'I'm drowning.'

'No, you're not.' Flipping onto his back, he kicked lazily away from her, still maintaining eye contact.

He was utterly heartless. She hit at the water surface angrily, sending a spray of silver droplets his way. None reached him, and she struck out towards him. Hannah was a reasonable swimmer but her efforts were severely hampered by her sodden clothes, and after a couple of feet she was puffing and panting.

'Stand up.'

Easy for him to say—he was ten feet tall! Cautiously she put a foot down. Her toe found the bottom, and, bouncing along for another few feet, she finally risked attempting to follow his advice.

The water reached her shoulder but it only reached Kamel's waist. He looked like a glistening statue—if cool stone had been capable of oozing the sort of restless vitality he projected. Kamel was not stone or cold. 'You did that deliberately!' she charged, focusing on her fury and not on his body—at least that was the aim.

When the sexiest man on the planet was standing there dripping wet and gorgeous it was hard to ignore.

He shrugged, fixing her with a gleaming amused gaze. 'What can I say? The temptation...' His voice trailed away as his glance dropped. The immersion had left her shirt plastered to her body; the lacy outline of her bra was clearly visible, as were the thrusting projections of her nipples. Heat pooled in his groin and the laughter faded from his heavy-lidded eyes as in his mind he saw himself drawing the ruched rosy peak into his mouth and heard her hoarse cry. He took a step towards her.

'Get away from me!' Refusing to recognise the heart-pounding excitement that made her feel light-headed, she banged the water with the heel of her hand in warning.

His response was a predatory smile. Holding out a hand to ward him off, she took a staggering step backwards and immediately sank beneath the surface. Floating on her back, kicking to stay afloat safely out of reach, she glared at him with eyes several shades deeper than the glittering water.

'That was so childish!' she accused, finding her feet again and stepping into marginally shallower water. 'I could have drowned—you'd have liked that.'

He arched a satiric brow. '*Me*, childish?'

Hannah blinked back at him, an expression of shock filtering into her eyes as their glances connected and locked. Her jaw dropped and her eyes widened as she thought, He's right. Who was the person who had charged in all guns blazing? She turned her glance downwards over her drenched clothes, and felt the clutch of cold, horrified embarrassment in her stomach. This wasn't her. She lifted her eyes, saw the way he was looking at her, and the cold in her belly turned hot and liquid.

'You're right. It is me!' she yelled. The discovery was liberating.

Kamel didn't have a clue what she was talking about and he didn't ask, because she was churning the water, windmilling her hands, sending as much spray over herself as him—and he reciprocated.

Hannah threw herself into the exertion and was not even aware of the point when she began to cry. Blinded by the spray, she didn't realise until her arms and shoulders got too tired to retaliate that Kamel had stopped splashing and he was standing right there, toe to toe with her.

The sun and the water droplets on her lashes gave a shimmering effect to his dark outline.

Everything seemed to slow, even her heartbeat. Her throat closed over, then she stopped breathing completely. She closed her eyes and felt his finger on her cheek. Leaking control from every pore, she opened her eyes. The sexual tension humming in the air had a stronger physical presence than the Mediterranean sun burning down on them.

'Are you crying?'

She shook her head, and wondered how he could tell.

'Come here!' he growled.

Afterwards, Hannah had no clue whether she stepped into him or whether he pulled her into his arms. All she knew was that it felt gloriously right to be there. His dark, hot eyes made her feel light-headed but she couldn't look away as he brushed the strands of wet hair away from her face. She couldn't take her eyes off him.

Kamel watched through eyes narrowed against the sun as the sparkling defiance faded from her blue eyes. He saw the hot glaze of desire drift in, and heard the husky little catch as she drew in a shuddering sigh and reached for his hand—not to pull it away, but to hold it there.

Kamel felt a rise of unfamiliar emotion as he looked down at her, and his fingers tightened around the slim ones that were entwined within his. He felt her shiver and frowned.

'You're cold.'

She shook her head. Turning her face into his palm, she felt anything but cold—she was burning from the inside out. She let out a gasp as Kamel dragged her into his body; the hard imprint of his erection against the softness of her belly drew another gasp, this one fractured. Her hands slid around the nape of his neck into his dark hair.

'Can I be of—?'

Kamel swore and cut across Rafiq's enquiry. 'No, we are fine. That will be all.'

The man bowed and melted away.

'You have a beautiful mouth,' she said, staring dreamily at the sculpted outline.

Kamel's face was a rigid mask of driven need as he brought his beautiful mouth crashing hungrily down on her soft, parted lips. Hannah's mind blanked as she went limp in his arms, giving herself over completely to the hungry, sensual onslaught of his deep, draining kisses. It felt as though he would drink her dry and she didn't mind one bit. She wanted it.

They were both breathing like sprinters crossing the line when he lifted his head. 'I can't get enough of you,' he confessed huskily.

'You make it sound like a bad thing,' she whispered.

He stroked her face, pulling her in even closer, feeling her breathing become more ragged as he let her feel how much he wanted her. 'Does that feel bad?' he asked.

'Oh, God, Kamel!' It was agony to be this close and yet not close enough, not nearly close enough. 'I feel...you're...' Her moan was lost inside his mouth.

It wasn't until they reached the edge of the pool and she saw her shirt floating on the water that Hannah realised that she was naked from the waist up.

How did that happen? She didn't spend long wondering. Consumed by an elemental hunger that allowed no room for thought, just feeling—layer and layer of hot feeling!—she plastered her aching, swollen breasts up hard against his chest and wound her legs tight around his waist, almost lifting herself clear of the water as she probed Kamel's mouth with her tongue, drawing a deep groan from his throat.

'Just hold on…let me…' He unwound her hands from around his neck, breaking the tenacious grip as he pushed her away from him.

'No…!' She opened her eyes and collided head-on with the heat in his.

Evading the hands that grabbed for him, Kamel spanned her waist with his hands and lifted her out of the water onto the edge of the pool. A moment later he was beside her, pulling her to her feet.

He lifted her into his arms and began to stride off—not in the direction of the villa, but the grassy area where a tree-lined stream ran through the sloping manicured lawn towards the deep forested area that bordered three sides of the property.

'We can't here…someone will see,' she protested half-heartedly.

'This is a paparazzi-free zone, I promise.'

'I wasn't thinking of intruders. People work here.'

She admired his confidence, and because he was kissing her like a starving man she allowed herself to be convinced by it. The simple truth was that she couldn't have stopped even if she had wanted to. And she didn't.

The grass he laid her on was soft against the bare skin of her back; the sun shining through the leafy canopy above left a dappled pattern on her skin. She lay breathing hard, one arm curved above her head, and anticipation made her stomach muscles quiver as he knelt beside her.

He bent forward, his body curving over hers, every muscle in his body pulled taut as he allowed the image to imprint on his retinas. It was one he knew would stay with him. The hectic flush of arousal on her cheeks, the wanton invitation that curled her soft full lips upwards—she was sinful temptation personified and it would take a stronger man than he was to resist.

Kamel had no intention of resisting; he just wanted to claim what was his, driven by primitive instincts as old as man.

He could feel her eyes on him as he slid the saturated skirt down her hips. His actions were made clumsy by the urgency that burned in his blood and the thin threads of lace on the tiny pants snapped as he tried to free her of the bondage.

Stripped of everything, her body was smooth and pale—so perfect that he couldn't breathe. He touched her breasts, running his thumbs across the tight peaks before he cupped them in his big hands.

Hannah closed her eyes, focusing everything on the sensation as he ran his hands over the smooth curve of her stomach, feeling the light calluses on his palms.

She raised her arms, reaching out towards him.

Eyes blazing with a need that made him shake, he knelt astride her, then, holding her eyes, he parted her thighs. Her skin was cool to the touch but inside she was hot. He closed his eyes and thrust in deeply, not holding back as he felt her hotness, her wetness close around him.

He ran a hand down her smooth thigh. 'Hold me now.'

Her long legs wrapped around him, locking around his waist to hold him as they pushed together towards a release that left them both breathless.

As Hannah gasped her way to cogent thought one surfaced, rising above the others, swirling in her pleasure-soaked brain. For that, she would do *anything*.

Even share him?

Everything in her said that was wrong. Self-disgust curled in the pit of her stomach.

But what was the alternative? Could there be room for compromise?

'I understand that there will be women.' The truth hurt, but she had to be grown up about this. 'I suppose I should not have reacted. If you—'

'Do not say it.' The cool command cut across her hesitant voice. 'I do not need your blessing to sleep with other women.'

She sucked in a taut breath. 'I know you don't need my permission,' she admitted unhappily.

He lifted his head from her breast, struggling against outrage even though a short time ago he would have welcomed her adult attitude. 'Only you could say something like that at a time like this. I am not thinking about other women every second of the day. I am thinking of you. And right now I am thinking of doing this again in bed. Would you prefer to talk or make a baby?'

'But I thought you wanted—'

'How could I know what I want when you insist on telling me? Come with me and I will tell you what I want.'

'That's a plan,' she agreed faintly.

CHAPTER ELEVEN

IT WAS ON the second night of their honeymoon that the telephone rang in the middle of the night. Kamel shifted her off his dead arm and reached for the phone with the other.

'I have to go.'

'What's wrong?'

Kamel put the phone back on the hook. Under his tan he was ashen.

'Your uncle?'

He shook his head. 'No, not that, thank God.'

She was relieved for his sake. She knew how fond Kamel was of his uncle and had also worked out from a few things he had said that he was in no hurry to take the throne. In fact, she had the impression that Kamel inexplicably thought he was not good enough to fill his cousin's shoes.

The few times Kamel had mentioned his cousin, the qualities he said he had possessed—

the ones that made him the perfect heir apparent—were qualities that Kamel had too, in abundance!

'There has been an earthquake.'

Hannah gasped.

'Rafiq will stay here with you.'

'Good luck and take care,' she said, struggling to keep her emotions low-key but wishing he had asked her to come with him.

'It's on occasions like this that my uncle must feel the loss of Hakim. It was so senseless. It will never make any sense. He had the ability to—'

Hannah could no longer hold her tongue. 'I'm sure your cousin was a great guy and it's desperately sad he is gone, but I'm damned sure he wasn't perfect. If he had been, he wouldn't have stolen the woman you loved! You're as good as he was any day of the week! Your uncle is lucky to have someone so dedicated.'

There was a long silence, finally broken by his slow drawl.

'So the gossips have been talking? I suppose that was to be expected. Well, one thing they didn't tell you is the difference between me and

Hakim is that he *wanted* to be the king. I hate the idea. And he had Amira beside him for support and that made all the difference for him.' Kamel found that lately he was able to think about their incredible devotion to one another without feeling bitter or jealous. It was one burden he no longer carried.

She gasped as though he had struck her and glanced down expecting to see a blade protruding from between her ribs. 'And you have me.'

'Don't worry,' he said, totally misinterpreting her reaction and her flat tone. 'I'm not expecting you to hold my hand.' He paused and cleared his throat. 'Amira was brought up to this life, and she knew the pressures.'

Unable to see the desperate pain and longing she knew would be in his face, Hannah looked away, hearing Raini's words in her head. *A beautiful queen.*

'I may not understand being royal,' she admitted quietly, 'but I do understand that, even though you hate it…' she lifted her gaze to his face and gave a quick smile '…you still put everything into it. That makes you someone who will make a great king one day.' Under the rather intense scrutiny of his dark eyes, she coloured. 'A king should have a level of arrogance that would be unacceptable in any other job.'

This drew a laugh from Kamel, who dropped a kiss on her mouth. Their lips clung...for how many seconds she didn't know, but it was long enough for Hannah to know she had fallen in love. And the man she loved would only ever see her as a pale imitation of the love of his life.

A little over a month after the earthquake, which had not actually caused any loss of life but had flattened a power plant, Hannah was breakfasting alone. She was in no hurry, as the ribbon-cutting ceremony for the opening of a new school had been unexpectedly postponed. When she'd asked why, her secretary had been strangely evasive, but then she was probably reading things into the situation that weren't there.

Like today—just because no one had remembered her birthday didn't mean that she had no friends, that nobody would miss her if she weren't there.

Struggling to divert the self-pitying direction of her thoughts, she picked up her fork and toyed with the smoked salmon and fluffy scrambled egg on her plate. It looked delicious, it smelt delicious, but she was not hungry. Her lack of hunger had nothing whatever to do with the fact it was her birthday and nobody had remembered. Actually, there had been other days this week when she had not been able to face breakfast.

She put down her fork and reminded herself that she was not a child. Birthdays no longer had the same importance, though even last year her father, who always made a fuss of her, despite the memories the day brought back for him—or perhaps because of them—had invited her friends for a pamper spa day. Hannah had known but she had pretended to be surprised.

Practically speaking you could hardly have a spa day with friends who were hundreds of miles away—and her father, it seemed, had forgotten. Out of sight, out of mind? She had rung him two nights on the run and he hadn't picked up or responded to her text messages. Presumably he had decided she was Kamel's problem now. And Kamel had left their bed at some unearthly hour. She had barely been able to open her eyes when he had kissed her and said, 'See you later.'

'How later?' she had muttered, wondering how he managed to expend so much energy during the night and still look fresh and dynamic in the morning. Would she have traded a fresh morning face for the nights of shared passion? Hannah hadn't even asked herself the question. It was a no-brainer.

The prospect of lying in Kamel's arms at night was what made the long and sometimes exhausting days bearable. It had been a steep learning curve and a shock to find herself with a personal secretary and a diary of official engagements. And part of the problem was of her own making. Initially, despite being advised to be cautious by her advisor, Hannah had agreed to lend her name to any worthy cause that approached her. Now she was snowed under by obligations to promote the numerous good causes she had lent her name to, and had been forced to be a little more discriminating.

Not only had she learnt her own life was not to be one of leisure, she had stopped thinking of Kamel's life as one of glitter and self-indulgence. He worked harder than anyone she had ever known, and as for glamour—some of what he was called upon to do was mind-numbingly boring and the flip side of that was the delicate tightrope of diplomacy he trod when he negotiated with men of power and influence.

He never complained, and she never told him how much she admired him. He had never mentioned Amira again but she was still there, the silent invisible presence. They could close the door on the rest of the world at the end of the day, but not his dead love. She was a constant. A perfect ideal that Hannah knew she could never live up to. She also worried about what would happen when those forbidden words slipped out in a moment of passion—so she really struggled to stay in control when they made love. Maybe Kamel guessed what she was doing because sometimes he looked at her oddly.

How would he react? she wondered, picking up her coffee cup. She had taken a sip from the cup before she saw what was concealed behind it: a gold-embossed envelope with her name inscribed in a bold familiar print across it.

She slopped coffee on the pristine white cloth in her haste to tear it open. It did not take long to read the message on the card inside.

Your birthday present is in the kitchen.

He knew it was her birthday and he'd bought her something! Like the child she no longer was, she leapt to her feet with a whoop of delight.

The private jet stood idling. Bad weather had delayed Kamel's flight. These things happened, and there was always a choice. A man could stress about a situation that was outside his control, fret and fume, and metaphorically or possibly literally bang his head against a brick wall.

Or he could not.

Kamel saved his energy for situations he could influence, but today he had struggled to retain this philosophical outlook. By the time his car drove through the palace gates it was almost

midnight and he was in a state of teeth-clench-
ing impatience.

He had bought women presents before, typi-
cally expensive baubles, and he took their appreciation for granted. The bauble he had bought
Hannah had been in a different class. News of
the record-breaking price it had fetched at auction had made the news headlines.

It had been a fortnight ago, the same night
that Kamel, who normally worked in his office
after dinner, had found himself wondering what
Hannah did while he worked. He spent each and
every night with her, he saw her in the morning
and her personal secretary told him what her
schedule was for the day. Sometimes they ate
together in the evening but after that…? It had
not previously occurred to him to wonder what
she did with herself in the evenings.

So he asked.

'The princess takes a walk and usually spends
some time in the small salon. She enjoys watching television.'

'Television?'

Rafiq nodded. 'I believe she follows a cookery programme. Sometimes she reads...' Without any change of expression, he had somehow managed to sound reproachful as he added, 'I think she might be lonely.'

'That will be all.' Only a long relationship and a respect for the older man stopped him saying more, but Kamel was incensed that his employee should think it came within his remit to tell him he was neglecting his wife!

If she was lonely, all she had to do was tell him. The trouble was that she had no sense, and could not accept advice. She had taken on an excessive workload, despite his giving her secretary explicit instructions to keep her duties light. She had ignored him, she had... His anger left him without warning, leaving him exposed to the inescapable fact that he had been guilty of neglect. Outside the bedroom he actively avoided her. But then logically if they were to be parents there would, for the child's sake, need to be some sort of mutual understanding outside the bedroom.

Lonely. A long way from home and anyone she knew, living in a totally foreign environment by a set of rules that were alien to her. And Kamel had needed someone to tell him that?

She hadn't complained and he had been happy and even relieved to take her seeming contentment at face value. Determined to make up for his neglect, he had gone to see for himself, but any expectation of discovering a forlorn figure had vanished when he'd walked into the small salon and found Hannah sitting cross-legged on a sofa giggling helplessly at the screen. She seemed surprised to see him but not interested enough to give him all her attention. Most of that remained on the television. Of course, it was a relief to discover she didn't need him to entertain her.

'A comedy?' He sat on the sofa arm and looked around. The room was one that he rarely entered but he recognised there had been some changes. Not just the television and bright cushions, but where a large oil painting had stood there was now a row of moody monochrome framed photographs of rugged mountain landscapes.

On the desk there was a piece of driftwood

and some shells beside an untidy stack of well-thumbed paperback novels.

Hannah caught him looking. 'The painting made me depressed and the other stuff is in a cupboard somewhere.'

'What a relief. I thought you might have pawned it.'

She looked at him as though she couldn't decide if he was joking or not. 'Do not let me interrupt your comedy.'

'It's a cookery competition. His sponge sank.'

'And that is good?'

She slung him a pitying look and shook her head. 'If he doesn't pull it out of the bag with his choux buns he's out.'

Kamel had stayed, not because he found the competitive side of baking entertaining, but because he found Hannah's enjoyment contagious. She was riveting viewing. It fascinated him to watch her face while she willed on her favourite, the sound of her throaty chuckle was entrancing, and her scolding of a contestant who, as she put it, *bottled it*, made him laugh.

When the programme finished he was sitting

beside her, sharing the sofa, and it was too late to go back to work. So he accepted her suggestion of a second glass of wine and watched a documentary with her. It was then he discovered that Hannah, renowned for her icy control, cried easily and laughed even more easily. Her aloof mask concealed someone who was warm, spontaneous and frighteningly emotional.

She had been pretending to be someone she wasn't for so long that he wondered if she remembered why she had developed the mask. But then his research into the subject had said that dyslexics developed coping mechanisms.

After that first evening it had become a habit for him to break from work a little earlier and join her. On the night he had taken receipt of her birthday gift he had cut his evening work completely and when he'd entered the salon had been feeling quite pleased with himself as he'd contemplated her reaction when she opened her gift the following week.

'No cookery programme?'

'No,' she'd snuffled, looking up at him through

suspiciously red eyes. 'It's too early. This is an appeal for the famine.'

The appeal had been followed by a news programme where the headline was not the famine but an item on the diamond purchased at auction by an anonymous buyer and the record-breaking price it had achieved.

When she'd expressed her condemnation of a society where the values were so skewed that people put a higher price on a shiny jewel than they did on children's lives, he'd agreed whole-heartedly with her view before going away to pass the ring he'd bought for her on to the next highest bidder, and to make a sizeable donation to the famine appeal. He'd then spent the rest of the evening wrestling with the problem of what the hell to buy for the woman who could have everything and didn't want it!

For a man who had never put any thought into a gift beyond signing a cheque it had not been easy, but he considered his solution inspired.

Would Hannah?

At some point he would have to ask himself why pleasing her mattered so much to him, but that remained a question for tomorrow. Today things were going rather well. This marriage could have been a total disaster but it wasn't.

The sound of music as he walked into the apartment drew him to the salon. A soft, sexy ballad was playing. The room was empty but the doors of the balcony were open and the dining table there was laid for two, with red roses and candles. The roses were drooping, the candles in the silver candelabra had burnt down, spilling wax on the table, and the champagne in the ice bucket was empty, as were the plates.

He was making sense of the scene when Rafiq appeared.

'Where?'

'I believe they are in the kitchen.'

'They?'

'The chef is still here.'

Rafiq opened the kitchen door, but neither his wife nor the celebrity chef he had flown in to give her a day's one-to-one teaching session heard him. Could that have had something to do with the open bottle of wine and two glasses on the table?

Or the fact they were having a great time? The guy with his fake smile and spray tan was relating an incident with enough name-dropping to make the most committed social climber wince.

Hannah wasn't wincing, though, she was eating it up, with her amazed gasps and impressed ahhs.

Well, she wasn't lonely, and she certainly wasn't missing him.

Scowling, he tugged at his tie and walked inside. He was paying the man to give his wife cooking lessons. He could manage the other things himself.

'Happy birthday.'

At the sound of the voice she had been waiting to hear all evening, Hannah's head turned. She started to her feet just in time, restraining the impulse to fling herself at him.

To his mind, her reaction had all the hallmarks of guilt.

'Have you had a good day?' His eyes slid to the chef, who had risen slowly to his feet.

'Yes, thank you.'

Her response and her demure, hand-clasped attitude reminded him of a child summoned to the headmaster's study, and he felt his temper rise.

'I made us a meal but you—'

'You missed a great meal, really great. This girl is a talent.'

'The girl is my wife.' Kamel had spent the day being pleasant to idiots but enough was enough.

'Hannah is a great pupil. Really talented.'

'Yes, you mentioned that. Well, thank you for stepping into the breach, but I would like to say happy birthday to my wife—alone. Shall I have someone show you to your room or can you—?'

'I'll be fine. Goodnight, all.'

The door closed and Hannah gave a sigh of relief. 'Thank goodness for that.'

Her reaction sent his antagonism down several levels.

'You did not enjoy your birthday present?'

'It was the best birthday present I have ever had! It was fine before he started drinking and then…' She shook her head. 'He kept telling the same story over and over and I couldn't get rid of

him. Thank goodness you came when you did.
I was ready to hide in the pantry, but at least it
stopped me brooding. Dad didn't call. I hope
he's all right. Some years he is worse than others,' she admitted, worriedly.

Kamel shook his head. *'Worse?'*

'Sorry, I was talking as if you knew.'

Kamel struggled to contain his frustration. He
had to drag every bit of information out of her.
'I would like to know.'

'My mother died when I was born. Well, actually she died a few weeks earlier. She was brain
dead but they kept her alive until I was strong
enough to be delivered. Dad stayed by her side
night and day all that time and when I was born
they switched off the life support. It's hardly any
wonder it was months before he could even look
at me. If it hadn't been for me she'd be alive.'

The fist around his heart tightened as she
raised her swimming blue eyes to him.

'Your father doesn't blame you for your mother's death.' No father could do that to an innocent child. It was more likely, knowing Hannah,

that she blamed herself. How had he ever thought this woman was selfish and shallow?

'Well, if he did I guess he's been trying to make up for it ever since by spoiling me rotten. I wish he'd ring.'

'Your father will be fine.'

Hannah nodded and stood there noticing the lines of fatigue etched into his face. Presumably he'd had a bad day—the same bad day that was responsible for the air of menace he had been radiating when he'd walked in. He'd made her think of a big panther, all leashed violence and tension.

'Come here.'

The rough invitation and the glow in his eyes made her tummy flip. 'Why?'

'I want to make up for missing your birthday.' He wanted to make up for every moment of pain in her life.

'What did you have in min—?' She let out a shriek as he scooped her up into his arms. 'What are you doing?'

He kicked open the door and grinned. 'I am taking you upstairs to give you the rest of your birthday present. It might,' he added, his eyes darkening as they swept her face, 'take some time.'

CHAPTER TWELVE

HANNAH KICKED OFF her shoes as she walked
into the bedroom. Kamel stood, his shoulders
propped against the door jamb, and watched as
she sat at the dressing table and struggled with
the clasp of the sapphire necklace she wore.

He had never imagined that the nape of a woman's neck could be erotic, but he had to accept
that some of life's normal rules did not apply
where his wife was concerned. When she had
walked into the room at his side tonight, making him think of a graceful swan in her slim-
fitting white gown, she had been literally shaking with fear but nobody would have guessed as
she smiled and charmed everyone present at the
formal state dinner.

The fierce pride he had felt as he had watched
her across the table, graceful and lovely, had
only been matched in the emotional stakes by

the rush of protectiveness he had experienced when, during the press-the-flesh session following the formal banquet, when those who were being rewarded for good works got a chance to meet the royals, Hannah's interest in the diverse range of people who lined up to shake her hand had seemed real—as had the fear in her eyes when she had seen the Quagani colonel. The moment had passed and she had recovered her poise, but Kamel had kept an eye on the man. Diplomatic incident or not, he was poised to throw the guy out personally if he so much as looked at Hannah the wrong way.

In the event he had seemed to behave himself. Even so, Kamel intended to make damned sure that in the future their favourite cuddly colonel had his card marked when it came to entry into this country.

'Let me.'

She looked at him in the mirror, unable to disguise the shiver of pleasure as his fingers brushed her neck.

'Thank you,' she said, looking at him through

her lashes with eyes that shone brighter than the gems he was removing.

He paused. She seemed about to say something but then, as if she had changed her mind, she tipped her head in acknowledgement as he dropped the necklace into her hand.

'You did well tonight.'

The comment smoothed the small groove in Hannah's brow and she released the sigh she'd felt she had been holding in all night. 'So I passed?'

He didn't return her smile. 'Is that how you saw tonight? As a test?' The idea troubled him. 'You're not being graded, Hannah. No one is judging you.'

Hannah shrugged. She had been here long enough to learn a little of the politics of the place, and she knew that she was resented in certain quarters. More than a few people were just waiting for her to mess up. She would never be Amira, but she was determined to prove them all wrong.

'Especially not me.'

Whatever trust issues he had with Hannah

had long gone. He often watched her—which was not exactly a hardship—and found himself wondering how he had ever even for a second thought she was a cold, spoilt bitch!

He was not a man who looked deep inside himself, maybe because he knew that he wouldn't have liked what he'd have seen.

He'd once told Hannah to lose the attitude, but now he saw that it was advice he ought to have been directing at himself. He'd seen marriage as a life sentence the moment when the doors slammed shut. He had not faced his resentment of the role that had been thrust on him. Hannah had made him do that.

He'd never for one second thought that marriage might be better than the life he'd had to let go. He'd put so much effort into seeing himself as someone who had missed out on the chance of happiness when he had lost Amira that when it had fallen at his feet he'd not recognised it.

And yet there was a cloud. Hannah welcomed him into her bed but he sensed a new restraint in her. She was holding back. On more than one occasion he had nearly demanded to know what the hell was the matter—but he'd stopped himself. What if she told him and he didn't like the answer?

His quiet admission that he hadn't been judging her made her throat ache with unshed tears.

'I was dreading it,' she admitted.

'I know.'

'It was strange sitting next to the man who once held my fate in his hands.' Protocol dictated that she was seated next to the daunting Sheikh Malek. 'He could have signed my death warrant.'

'No!'

The explosive interjection made her pause and touch his hand. His fingers unclenched under the light pressure. 'Tonight he was telling me about his rose collection. He invited me to a tour of his rose gardens.'

Kamel let out a silent whistle as he brought his hands up to rest on her shoulders. 'You're honoured. I haven't made that invite yet. It's the hottest ticket in town, I promise you.'

He bent his head and Hannah closed her eyes, but the anticipated kiss did not arrive on her waiting lips. With a disgruntled little frown between her feathery brows, she opened her eyes and saw him digging into the pocket of his jacket.

'I almost forgot. This is yours, I believe.'

Her frown deepened as she shook her head and looked at the small fat brown envelope he held. 'It's not mine.'

He turned it over. 'Well, it's got your name on the front.'

Sliding her finger under the sealed flap, she split it open and angled a questioning look up at him, suspecting this was Kamel's way of delivering a surprise. 'There's no celebrity chef hiding inside, is there?'

Kamel responded to the teasing with a lopsided grin. 'The man's ego wouldn't fit into this room, let alone an envelope.'

Hannah turned the parcel around, feeling an odd reluctance suddenly to open it. 'Where did it come from?'

'Someone saw you drop it, handed it to someone who passed it on to me. I assumed it fell out of your bag.'

Her lips quirked into an amused smile. 'My bag will just about hold a lipstick.'

Her explanation drew a puzzled look. 'Then why carry it?'

'Only a man would ask that question.'

'What is it?' he asked as she tipped the contents of the envelope onto the dressing table.

'I've no idea,' she admitted, staring as several photos clipped together fell out, then, after another shake, a card. 'It says here that…' She read the logo on top of the card and her brows lifted. 'Private investigator!'

Kamel picked up the photos. He did not look beyond the one on the top. A muscle in his lean cheek clenched.

'What's wrong?' she asked, struggling to read his shuttered expression.

'See for yourself.' He slid the clip off the bundle and fanned them out, playing-card style, on the surface in front of her.

Hannah accepted the invitation, and the nausea she had been feeling intermittently all evening resurfaced with a vengeance. There were two people in each grainy print and, even though they had clearly been taken using a telephoto lens and there was some graininess, there was no mistaking one at least of the faces…or the body.

Kamel's mouth twisted in distaste.

'I thought we had all of these.'

Of course, once images made their way onto the Internet they were there for ever, but the person who had taken these had been refreshingly pragmatic. The only thing he'd been interested in was money, not causing embarrassment.

'You knew about these?' She held a clenched fist to her pale lips.

'These were taken long before we were married. You do know that, don't you?' He could have pointed out that the dress she was wearing—when she was wearing one—was the gold number that had been the trigger for their poolside tussle. But he shouldn't have to.

He had not needed to ask Hannah if she had employed a private investigator; he knew she hadn't. He recognised this for what it was—a rather obvious and malicious attempt at mischief-making, one that could only work in a marriage where there was a lack of trust that could be exploited.

'Do you believe me, Hannah? Do you trust me?'

Saying she did amounted to an admission that she loved him. Was she ready to make it?

The realisation that she was came hand in hand with the even stronger realisation that if she didn't move fast she was going to throw up all over his shiny shoes.

She threw him an agonised look, then dashed to the bathroom with her hand pressed to her lips, and slammed the door in his face.

When she finished being violently sick, Hannah got weakly to her feet and washed her face. A look in the mirror told her she looked like death warmed up. She went back into the bedroom.

She squared her shoulders and opened the door. It was time she manned up and came clean. She would tell him that, not only did she trust his word, she trusted him with her life and that of their unborn baby.

She curved a protective hand over her flat belly and whispered, 'Here goes.'

It was empty.

The anticlimax was intense, but it only lasted a moment. She looked back on their conversation before she had made her dash for the bathroom, and she saw the situation from his perspective. He had asked her if she trusted him and she had bolted.

She put herself in his shoes—what was he thinking?

The answer was not long coming. He thought she didn't trust him. The knowledge buzzed in her head and she knew it wouldn't go away until she told him how she felt.

He had to know she wasn't that person. Fuelled by an urgency that infected every cell of her body, that defied logic, she ignored the heels she had kicked off and shoved her feet into a pair of trainers.

The bodyguard standing outside the door moved to one side as she exploded through the door.

'Where is he?'

The steely face betrayed a concern as he looked down at her.

'Shall I get someone for you—?'

'No, just tell me where he went!' she screeched, fighting the impulse to beat her hands on his chest.

After a pause that seemed to Hannah to go on for ever, he nodded to the door that led to the stone spiral steps that in turn led to the side entrance to their apartment.

Hannah's grateful smile shone, causing the big man to blush but she didn't notice. Slinging a 'Thank you!' over her shoulder, she flew down the stairs at record-breaking speed, slowing only when she remembered the baby.

Outside her burst of optimism vanished as she scanned the surrounding area lit by spotlights. Her anxious gaze failed to pick up any sign of movement amongst the rows of fragrant lemon trees that grew in the manicured expanse of green, a green maintained by high-tech underground irrigation.

She was about to concede defeat when she saw a figure who had been previously concealed by a hollow in the undulating ground outlined on the horizon.

'Kamel!'

Maybe he didn't hear her, or maybe he chose to ignore her. Her jaw firmed; she'd *make* him listen, she told herself grimly, or die in the attempt!

In her head she could hear him calling her a drama queen. Tears welled in her eyes and she tried to call his name but nothing came out of her mouth. Swallowing tears and the frustration that lay like a weight in her chest, she willed herself on.

He had vanished from view before she had made it halfway across the grass, but when she reached the top of the rise she had a lucky break: she saw his tall figure enter the massive garage block.

With cruel timing as she came around the building a sports car emerged through the open doors, kicking up a cloud of dust that made her cough as it vanished.

Well, that was it.

Feeling utterly deflated, she stopped to catch

her breath, pressing her hand to a stitch in her side. She experienced a moment's panic before telling herself not to be stupid. Pregnant women played sport, rode horses, did things a lot more physically demanding than jog a few hundred yards. Her only problem was she was unfit.

Actually it wasn't her only problem. Why had she hesitated? If she had told him how she felt he wouldn't have needed to be told she trusted him. He'd have known. But, no, she'd been busy covering her back, protecting herself from the man who, whether he had intended to or not, had shown her what love was about.

It had been weeks since she'd admitted it to herself and she'd been too scared to let him see she loved him. She was disgusted by her own cowardice. Maybe it was only sex for him, but she had to know. She *needed* to know. She needed to tell him she was alive and Amira was dead. She had to be brave for their baby.

Hands braced on her thighs, she leant forward to get her breath. It was time to be honest. If she didn't it would be her own insecurity that stretched the gulf that had opened up between them tonight.

She was so caught up with her own internal dialogue that as she straightened up and brushed the hair back from her face she almost missed the figure that emerged from the garage block, the figure carrying the cane. The figure of the colonel...

For a moment literally paralysed with fear, Hannah felt herself dragged back to that room of her nightmares—the bright white light, the stains on the wall that she didn't like to think about and the sinister tap, tap of that cane.

But he wasn't tapping his stick. He wasn't doing anything to attract attention to himself. As he moved towards the staff quarters he looked furtively left and right, then over his shoulder. For a moment he seemed to be looking straight at her and, standing there in the pale ball gown, she felt as though there were a neon arrow above her head. Then he turned and walked away quickly.

It was only after he had vanished that she began to breathe again.

She was ashamed that she'd felt so afraid. He

couldn't hurt her any more. He never had; he'd only been playing mind games. He was harmless really. But harmless or not, remembering the expression she had caught a glimpse of earlier that evening when his cold little eyes had followed Kamel across the room made her shudder.

'Hannah, you're way too old to believe in the bogey man.' Firmly ejecting the hateful little creep from her head, Hannah was turning to retrace her steps when she lost her footing. By some miracle she managed not to fall, but she did jar her ankle. Flexing her toes and extending her foot to see the damage, she noticed a dark patch on the ground. There was a trail of similar spots leading all the way back to the garage. Unable to shake the feeling that something was not quite right, she found herself following the breadcrumb trail of spots. It led back into the large hangar of a building that housed Kamel's collection of cars.

She had seen them before and had made a few appropriate noises of approval, though in all honesty her interest in high-end vintage cars was limited. So long as the car she drove got her from A to B she was happy.

The lights were off in the building, but as she walked inside the internal sensor switched them on, revealing the rows of gleaming cars inside. Only one was absent—the vintage sports car that Kamel had driven off in. Where it had stood in the empty space the trail came to an end.

While Hannah's interest in cars was limited, a condition of her being given driving lessons for her seventeenth birthday had been she attend some basic car-maintenance classes. Some things had stuck with her, like the unpleasant smell of brake fluid.

She dipped her finger in the pool, lifted it to her nose and gave a whimper, the colour fading from her face. The images clicked through her head. The hate in that man's eyes, his furtive manner as he'd left the building. Why hadn't she challenged him? Would the little coward dare...?

She didn't follow the line of speculation to its conclusion; she didn't think of the security guard who might have kept a discreet distance but was undoubtedly within calling distance, or even the internal phone on the wall behind her. She just ran.

The palace compound was more like a village or small town than a single residence, and, though it was possible to take a direct route to the heavy entrance gates, there was also a more circuitous route. She had complained recently that Kamel treated it as if it were his own private racing track. He had laughed when she'd closed her eyes and squealed at the last hairpin bend, convinced they were heading straight into a wall.

Without brakes... She shook her head to clear the image and pushed on. On foot it was possible to take a much shorter, direct route. She ought to be able to cut him off before— She refused to think that she was not going to make it in time.

The information did not make it to her lungs. They already felt as though they were going to explode and when she was forced to stop to catch her breath it also gave her body time for the pain in her ankle to register. That was when she remembered the phone in the garage block. She could have rung through to the entrance gate—someone would be there now, ready to warn Kamel. She was trying to decide between the options of going back to the phone or trying to intercept him when she saw a really ancient bike propped up against a wall.

Sending up a silent thanks to whoever had left it there, she climbed aboard and began to pedal through the trees.

Kamel had gunned his way out of the garage.

It all happened so fast the sequence of events was a blur: the car appearing, throwing herself into the road, arms waving, then the crunch of metal as the front of the Aston Martin embedded itself into a tree.

I've killed him!

She felt empty, her body was numb—and then the door of the car was being wrenched open. It actually fell off its hinges as Kamel—large, very alive and in what appeared to be a towering rage—vaulted from the vehicle. The feeling rushed back and she began to laugh and cry at the same time.

'You little fool! What the hell were you doing?

I could have killed you!' Looking white and shaken and a million miles from his indestructibly assured self, Kamel took her roughly by the shoulders and wrenched her around to face him. He registered the tears sliding down her face and hissed out a soft curse. How could you yell at someone who looked like that? 'You just took ten years off my life.' If he had no Hannah he would have no life; the blinding insight stretched his self-control to the limit.

'I had to stop you—the car, the brakes...'

His ferocious frown deepened. 'How the hell did you know about the brakes?'

She wiped the tears from her cheeks with the back of one hand and sniffed. 'You knew?'

'I stopped a few yards after I left the garage.' To ask himself what the hell he was doing. Throwing some sort of tantrum because she didn't immediately express unconditional trust? He'd moved the goalposts of this relationship on an almost daily basis. Hell, at the start, he hadn't even wanted a relationship. If he had to work for her trust, he would. 'Or tried to.' He had used the gears to slow down to a crawl, planning to pull over at an appropriate place, which was the only reason he had not hit Hannah.

He closed his eyes and swallowed, reliving the nightmare moment when she had rushed into the road.

'So you knew about what he tried to do?'

'Who tried to do what?'

'The colonel. He cut your brakes and I think he might be the one who sent the photos.'

Understanding softened his dark eyes as he placed a thumb under her chin, tilting her tear-stained face up to him. 'Really sweetheart, that man can't hurt you and I promise you will never have to see him again.'

She pulled away from him. 'No!' she gritted emphatically through clenched teeth. 'Don't look at me like that, and don't even think about humouring me. I am *not* imagining things and it was *you* he was trying to hurt. You humiliated him. I saw the way he looked at you tonight, and then when I followed you he was in the garage and he didn't want to be seen. So when I saw the brake fluid I knew...' She pressed a hand to her chest and gulped back a sob and whispered, 'I had to stop you.'

'You were following me?'

'I just told you—someone tried to kill you.'

'I'll look into it. He will be brought to justice if he is guilty.' There was no hint of doubt in Kamel's voice. 'You followed me?'

She nodded.

'Why?' He hooked a finger under her chin and forced her to look at him, Hannah met his interrogative dark stare steadily, not trying to look away, feeling weirdly calm now the moment was here.

'Because you asked me a question and you left before I could answer.'

'You ran away.'

'It was that or throw up all over your shoes.'

He stiffened. 'You're ill?'

'Not ill.' For the first time she struggled to hold his gaze. 'You asked me if I trust you and the answer is yes, I do. Totally and absolutely. I know you always have my back—that's one of the things I love about you. Of course, there are an awful lot of things about you that drive me crazy but they don't matter because I love you...' She gave a quivering smile. It hadn't been as hard as she had anticipated, speaking the words that had been locked within her heart. 'The whole package. You.'

This was the moment when in her dreams he confessed his love for her. But this wasn't a dream; it was real. And he stood there, every muscle in his stark white face frozen, tension pulling the skin tight across the bones of his face.

Hannah walked into the wall of pain and kept going, her expression fixed in a reasonable mask. No matter how hard she wanted it, it just wasn't going to happen.

'It's all right. I know that love was not part of the deal. I know that Amira...you will always love her, but it doesn't have to be a deal breaker, does it?'

She felt the tension leave his body. 'Say it again. I want to hear it.'

The glow in his eyes was speaking not to her brain, which was counselling caution, but directly to her heart. It stopped and then soared, and she smiled.

'I love you, Kamel.' She left a gap and this time he filled it.

'*Je t'aime, ma chérie. Je t'aime.* I have been too stubborn, too scared to admit it to myself.'

'Amira…?'

'I loved Amira, and her memory will always be dear to me. But what I felt for her was a thing that… If I thought you loved another man I would not let you go to him. I would lock you up in a tower. I am jealous of everyone you smile at. That damned chef creep…'

'Jealous? You… You're not just saying that because of the baby?' She saw his expression and gave a comical groan. 'I didn't mention that part yet, did I?'

'Baby…there is a baby? Our baby?'

She nodded.

He pressed a hand to her stomach. 'You do know how much you have changed my life?'

'I thought that was exactly what you didn't want.'

He shrugged. 'I was a fool. And you were

charming and infuriating and brave and so beautiful. You swept into my life like a cleansing breeze, a healing breeze.'

He opened his arms and, eyes shining, she stepped into them, sighing as she felt them close behind her. 'I love you so much, Kamel. It's been an *agony* not saying it. It got so that I couldn't even relax properly when we made love—I was so scared of blurting it out.'

'So it was not that you had tired of me?'

She laughed at the thought. 'That is never going to happen.'

He put a thumb under her chin, tilting her glowing face up to him. 'You can say it as often as you wish now. In fact, I insist you say it.'

She was giggling happily as he swept her into his arms, and still when the security guard accompanied by a grim-faced Rafiq found them.

'Kamel, stop him. He's calling a doctor. Tell him I'm not ill,' she urged as her husband strode on, refusing her requests to be put down.

'You have had a stressful day and you are pregnant and I think it might be a good idea if a doctor gives you a check-over.'

'And I suppose it doesn't matter what I say?'

'No.'

She touched the hard plane of his lean cheek.

'You're impossible!' she said lovingly.

'And you are mine,' he said simply.

* * * * *

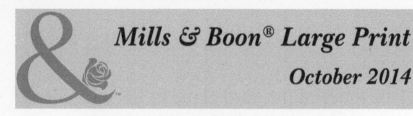

Mills & Boon® Large Print
October 2014

0914 Rom LP

Mills & Boon® Large Print
November 2014

CHRISTAKIS'S REBELLIOUS WIFE
Lynne Graham

AT NO MAN'S COMMAND
Melanie Milburne

CARRYING THE SHEIKH'S HEIR
Lynn Raye Harris

BOUND BY THE ITALIAN'S CONTRACT
Janette Kenny

DANTE'S UNEXPECTED LEGACY
Catherine George

A DEAL WITH DEMAKIS
Tara Pammi

THE ULTIMATE PLAYBOY
Maya Blake

HER IRRESISTIBLE PROTECTOR
Michelle Douglas

THE MAVERICK MILLIONAIRE
Alison Roberts

THE RETURN OF THE REBEL
Jennifer Faye

THE TYCOON AND THE WEDDING PLANNER
Kandy Shepherd

MILLS & BOON®

Why shop at millsandboon.co.uk?

Each year, thousands of romance readers find their perfect read at millsandboon.co.uk. That's because we're passionate about bringing you the very best romantic fiction. Here are some of the advantages of shopping at www.millsandboon.co.uk:

* **Get new books first**—you'll be able to buy your favourite books one month before they hit the shops

* **Get exclusive discounts**—you'll also be able to buy our specially created monthly collections, with up to 50% off the RRP

* **Find your favourite authors**—latest news, interviews and new releases for all your favourite authors and series on our website, plus ideas for what to try next

* **Join in**—once you've bought your favourite books, don't forget to register with us to rate, review and join in the discussions

Visit **www.millsandboon.co.uk**
for all this and more today!